MARRYING MR. WENTWORTH

AUSTEN HUNKS
BOOK THREE

VALERIE BOWMAN

JUNE THIRD ENTERPRISES, LLC

She wants nothing to do with him...

Ariana Remington has spent years building a life where no one can hurt her again. A brilliant prosecutor with a sharp tongue and an iron heart, she's made peace with her single status. But waking up in Las Vegas—married to her ex, Christopher Wentworth—was not part of the plan.

He wants a second chance.

Christopher has traded his reckless youth for stardom as a country rock musician, but fame and fortune haven't erased the one regret he carries: losing Ariana. Now fate has handed him an unexpected shot at redemption, and he's determined not to waste it.

Can a Vegas mistake become their forever?

Ariana's walls are high, and Christopher's decision still casts a long shadow. To turn their accidental marriage into a real one, they'll have to confront old wounds, trust new feelings, and decide if love deserves a second act.

CHAPTER 1

A Saturday in May — Milwaukee — Ariana

I stared at the group text like it personally offended me. Which, to be fair, it kind of did.

Meg:

> Vegas here we come! Less than one week til party time! Pack your party-pants people— Luke's jet leaves Thursday at noon!

There were heart emojis. A cowboy hat. A champagne bottle. Someone had even replied with a dancing Elvis. I reread it four times, hoping my phone might spontaneously combust and save me from what I was about to do.

Because the part Meg didn't mention?

Was that Christopher Wentworth would be on that plane.

The Christopher Wentworth.

My ex. My first love. My high school sweetheart turned college boyfriend turned absolute emotional wrecking ball. The man who broke my heart so cleanly, so suddenly, so surgically, it should've come with a hospital bill and a complimentary trauma counselor.

Also? He just so happened to be the bass guitarist for Whiskey Smoke. Which wasn't just a band. They were *the* band.

Billboard #1s. CMA awards. Sold-out arenas. Magazine covers. Streaming charts. Viral tours. You couldn't throw a rhinestone in Nashville without hitting some piece of Whiskey Smoke merch. And Christopher? His face—and abs—no doubt graced a thousand bedroom walls. His broody stage presence and boyish smirk had turned him into a walking, bass-playing thirst trap.

That Christopher.

I dropped my phone onto the kitchen counter like it had insulted my entire bloodline and reached for the nearest coffee mug. It still held yesterday's dregs. Appropriate.

The man had been out of my life for years, and now he was about to be on a private jet with me ahead of an entire weekend in Vegas, where everything was loud and glitzy and fueled by bad decisions and worse judgment.

I needed backup. This called for FaceTime.

I picked up the phone again and clicked my brother's number. Jeremy and his fiancée, Meg, had moved to Nashville recently. Jeremy was building a career as a custom woodworker, and Meg, a former history professor, was now writing historical romance novels full-time. I still missed them. FaceTime made it slightly better.

He answered on the third ring, FaceTime switching on to reveal him standing in his shop with some kind of sanding tool in one hand and guilt already written all over his face.

"Everything okay?" he asked, trying to sound casual. He'd seen the group text. He knew damn well everything was not okay.

"You knew about the jet," I said flatly.

He set the sander down like that was going to protect him. "Luke offered. He's got the jet. Figured it'd be more fun than a bunch of commercial flights."

"Uh-huh." I folded my arms. "And the part where *he's* going?"

Jeremy's face tightened like he was bracing for impact. "Luke wanted to invite the whole group. And he's...technically part of the group."

"He hasn't been part of *my* group since the Obama administration."

"Come on, Ari. It's been—what—ten years?"

"Eleven." Not that I was counting. (I was absolutely counting.)

Jeremy had the decency to look vaguely ashamed. "You don't have to talk to him. Just get on the plane, drink champagne, wear something sparkly, and pretend he doesn't exist."

Oh, sure. Just pretend the man who once made me believe in forever hadn't shattered me like a dropped wineglass. Easy peasy. "You make it sound simple."

Jeremy ran a hand over his face. He sighed. "Look, I get it. It's not ideal. But Meg wants you there. I want you there. And it's Vegas. It's not like you're gonna get trapped in an elevator with him."

"You say that like fate doesn't have a sick sense of humor."

I moved back to my laptop, closed the case file I'd been reading with a satisfying snap, and let the silence stretch between us.

Finally, I said, "Fine. I'll go. But if he even breathes near me, I'm invoking my right to disappear and fake my own death."

Jeremy smirked. "That's the spirit."

"I'm serious."

"I know." His smile softened. "Still glad you're coming."

I didn't respond. Because I *was* going. I was going to slap on a smile, toast my brother and his future wife, and pretend that being trapped on a jet at thirty thousand feet with the man who'd turned me into an emotional armadillo wasn't sending me into a full-blown cardiac episode.

But the truth?

The second I laid eyes on Christopher Wentworth again?

All bets were off.

CHAPTER 2

The same Saturday — Nashville — Christopher

I was halfway through a cold beer and a half-decent riff —one of those moody bass lines that might've turned into something if I'd stuck with it—when my phone lit up with a text from Remington.

JEREMY:

> Just a heads-up. Ariana's coming to Vegas next weekend. Luke's jet leaves at noon Thursday.

I stared at the screen for a solid minute, like maybe if I blinked hard enough, it would morph into something less catastrophic. Something like:

Just kidding, she's not coming.
Never mind—she moved to Siberia.

Ariana Remington has legally changed her name and joined a monastery in the Swiss Alps.

But no. The text remained stubbornly unchanged, glaring up at me in brutal clarity.

Ariana. Coming. Vegas.

I stood up too fast and knocked over my amp stool. The thud echoed across the room like karma.

"Shit."

Across the studio, Holt didn't even look up from his laptop. He was eating trail mix straight out of the bag, earbuds in, sunglasses on indoors like a man determined to keep the illusion of chill at all costs.

"You okay, bro?" he asked, not glancing up.

"No," I muttered, picking up the stool and setting it upright. "No, I am not okay."

"Why? The label screw something up again? Please tell me we don't have to re-record that chorus again. I will lose my mind—"

"She's coming to Vegas," I said.

That got his attention.

He pulled one earbud out. "The *she?*"

I gave him a look. The look. The one that said, *Don't even pretend you don't know who I'm talking about.*

Nick Holt, drummer and human meme generator, let out a low whistle. "Damn. What's it been, like, ten years?"

"Eleven," I said automatically.

He smirked. "And you still know the exact number. That's…alarmingly unhealthy."

I didn't answer. Just dropped onto the couch like someone had cut the strings holding me up and let my head fall back against the cushion. The ceiling fan above me spun lazily, unbothered. Must be nice.

"I didn't think she'd come," I said finally.

Nick shut his laptop and leaned back in the chair, lacing his fingers behind his head. "Why wouldn't she? She's Jeremy's sister. And Meg's best friend. She's in the wedding party. You? You're just the bandmate with emotional baggage."

"Yeah, thanks for that."

He shrugged. "Hey, I didn't say you weren't important. Just…less impossible to avoid."

"I figured if she knew I was going, she'd find an excuse," I said. "Some court thing. A 'can't miss' case. Sudden flu. Literally *anything*."

"Wait," Nick said, squinting at me. "You didn't want her to come?"

"No, I did. I do. I just…didn't expect it."

"Bro. That sounds like a line from a song you already wrote."

I ignored that. Mostly because he wasn't wrong.

Nick leaned forward, resting his elbows on his knees. "Alright. Walk me through this again. You and Ariana were what? High school sweethearts?"

"Yep."

"College couple?"

"Three years."

He narrowed his eyes. "Then what happened?"

"I happened."

He raised an eyebrow.

I sighed. "I ended it. Thought I was doing the right thing. Thought she needed to be free to go live her big life without dragging around a guy sleeping on couches and chasing record deals that paid in beer and exposure."

Nick didn't say anything. Just gave me that look—the one that said, *You already know you messed this up, so I won't pile on…much.*

The truth was that all the guys knew. Hell, anyone who'd toured with us in those early years knew. The ones who shared hotel rooms or vans or even those terrible little green rooms with the flickering fluorescent lights—they'd all heard the stories.

Because when I got drunk enough—and I usually did—I talked about Ariana.

Not in the past tense. Not like some ex I'd "learned a lot from." No. I talked about her like she was still there. Like she was waiting somewhere. Like I was going to open a door and find her sitting on the couch with a mug of tea and that sharp, skeptical eyebrow raised like *finally*.

Because in my head?

She *was* still there.

I never really let her leave. Not emotionally, anyway. She was frozen in time in my memory—twenty and brilliant and furious and mine. Except she wasn't anymore.

And now?

Now she was going to be real. In front of me. Breathing. Moving. Looking at me with those emerald eyes that could cut steel or seduce, depending on the day.

"You think she'll talk to me?" I asked, trying to make it sound casual.

Nick snorted. "Not unless it's to file a restraining order."

I groaned and let my head fall forward into my hands. "God. She *hates* me."

"And you're still in love with her."

I looked up. "Did I say that?"

"You didn't have to."

He stood, stretching like a man with no emotional crisis to shoulder. "Well, either way, this trip just got a lot more interesting. Hope you packed something bulletproof."

I leaned back, closed my eyes, and tried to breathe. Inhale. Exhale. Ignore the memory of how Ariana looked the last time I saw her—chin lifted, jaw clenched, eyes full of betrayal.

I hadn't meant to hurt her.

But I had.

And now?

Now I was going to have to face her in Vegas, where emotions were high, the champagne was unlimited, and the temptation to say the wrong thing was lurking in every shadow.

God help me.

Vegas just got a whole lot more dangerous.

CHAPTER 3

Wednesday morning — Milwaukee — Ariana

The lights in the courthouse were doing their usual impression of an interrogation room—harsh, fluorescent, and about as forgiving as a failed cross-examination. They flickered slightly as I stepped into the prosecutors' bullpen, projecting just enough of a buzz to grind directly against my last nerve.

I tugged at the collar of my blazer and walked in like I hadn't been awake since four a.m., reading depositions in bed with one hand while eating dry Cheerios out of the box with the other. Clutched against my chest was my latest case file— assault with a deadly weapon and more conflicting eyewitness testimony than a daytime courtroom show. I held it like a lifeline. Or maybe a shield.

The bullpen was already humming. Phones ringing. Keyboards clacking. Paper being shuffled with the kind of righteous urgency that only prosecutors and postal workers seemed to possess. The scent of burnt coffee, over-worn polyester suits, and late-stage capitalism filled the air. God, I almost missed it when I was gone.

"Morning, Remington."

Scott Landry's voice drifted over from the next desk, warm and easy, like a smile in vocal form. I glanced over and, yep, there it was—his trademark lazy grin. The kind that had probably charmed every admin, intern, and newly hired ADA since 2012. Tall, clean-cut, with eyes full of golden retriever sincerity and just enough edge to avoid being boring.

Theoretically, everything I should want.

"Hey," I said, dropping my bag beside my desk with a heavy thud and slumping into my chair like a woman emotionally carried in on a stretcher. "Busy docket?"

"Three pretrials and a sentencing. I heard your eight a.m. started off with some…poetry?"

I groaned and let my head thunk gently against my desk. "Defense counsel brought in a character witness who insisted on testifying in haiku. Actual. Haiku. I counted the syllables."

Scott chuckled. "Poetic justice."

I lifted my head just enough to shoot him a look. "If I hear one more legal pun before I finish this coffee, I swear to God, Scott—"

"Message received." He raised his hands in mock surrender.

He stood and wandered over, propping his elbow on the edge of my desk like we were starring in some kind of indie workplace rom-com, where he was the earnest suitor and I was the overworked, emotionally unavailable female lead with a tragic backstory and a complicated ex.

Which wasn't wrong.

"Did you see the email about guardian ad litem volunteers?" he asked, the grin softening. "They need more for the next intake."

I sighed. "Yeah. I saw it. Wish I could sign up."

He nodded. "Conflict of interest?"

"Exactly. Prosecutors aren't allowed. Not officially. Still kills me though. Those kids need someone. Someone who knows how the system works and gives a damn."

His expression changed—gone was the playfulness, replaced by something quieter. Sharper.

"I had one last year," he said. "Nine-year-old girl. Testified against her dad. Brave as hell. Didn't cry once. Sent me a Christmas card."

My chest tightened. "Jesus. Nine years old?"

"Yeah."

There was a beat. Long enough for the hum of the fluorescent lights to fill the silence between us. It didn't need words. We'd both seen it too many times—kids swallowed by a system built for bureaucracy, not mercy.

"They're just trying to survive," I said softly. "And we give them forms to fill out."

He nodded. "Hardest part of the job."

"Harder than murder trials?"

"Some days, yeah."

I looked down at the file in front of me, but the words blurred. Not from lack of sleep this time, but from the simple truth that no matter how many motions I filed or how many closing arguments I nailed, there were cracks in the system you couldn't seal with case law. And some days, that made me want to burn the whole thing down.

There was a pause. A charged one. The kind where the air thickens just slightly. Where you know what's coming, even before the words hit the air.

"So…" Scott began, voice casual. Too casual. "What about that drink I keep asking you about? Maybe this weekend?"

And there it was.

I smiled before I could stop myself. Automatic. Polished. Professional. "I can't. I'm going to Vegas."

"Ah," he said. "The bachelorette trip?"

"Yep. My brother's bachelor-slash-bachelorette weekend. Jet. Champagne. Emotional chaos, probably."

Scott nodded, trying to look nonchalant. But I caught it. That small flicker in his expression—the brief shadow of disappointment before it vanished under something more neutral. The man was good. He should've been a defense attorney.

"Another time, maybe," he said.

"Maybe," I echoed.

But we both knew what that meant. What it always meant. I wasn't going. Not really. Not ever.

Scott was smart. Funny. Kind. The kind of guy who remembered birthdays and sent thank-you notes and brought donuts on Fridays without trying to make a statement about it. The kind of man who showed up. Who *stayed*.

So why did I keep saying no?

I knew why.

Because I didn't trust "easy." Or at all, maybe. Because I'd already learned what happened when you handed your heart to someone and believed they'd keep it safe. Because once upon a time, I'd been all-in with someone who told me I was his future...and then walked away like it was nothing.

Christopher.

His name still did things to my pulse.

I turned back to the case file, determined to focus, to drown out the thought of him in paperwork and policy. But the words on the page were useless. Flat ink and legal jargon couldn't distract me from the fact that somewhere out there, he still existed. That he was going to be in Vegas. That I'd see him.

And not from a distance. Not in passing. Not on a magazine cover while I stood in line at the grocery store.

On a *private jet*.

At parties.

In photos.

In my proximity.

I hadn't seen him since that hallway outside my dorm room after junior year, where he ended us with the kind of finality usually reserved for death or life sentences. And yet, he never really left. Not from my memory. Not from my music library. Not from the dreams I woke up from with the ache of him still in my chest.

Every time someone got too close—Scott included—my heart pulled back. Like it remembered. Like it had a muscle memory of how it felt to get dropped mid-future.

Don't, it warned me. *It's not worth the fall.*

And maybe it wasn't. Maybe it was safer to be whole and lonely than shattered and in love.

But now? Here I was—steady job, decent apartment, good friends—still living a life that looked whole from the outside.

But some part of me hadn't healed.

Vegas was waiting.

And with it…the one man who'd caused all the trouble to begin with.

CHAPTER 4

Thursday at noon — Milwaukee Private Airport — Ariana

There are a few things you expect when you pull up to a private hangar for a bachelor-slash-bachelorette weekend in Vegas.

Champagne. Luggage the size of compact cars. A well-dressed assistant named Blaine or Reese asking if you'd like a lavender-scented eye mask for the flight.

What you do *not* expect—what no rational woman should ever have to endure—is climbing the stairs to a Gulfstream G700 and coming face to face with the man who broke your heart so cleanly it might as well have come with a discharge summary and a copy of your vitals.

Christopher @#$% Wentworth.

Of course he was already on the plane. And of course he looked even hotter than before.

Because fate isn't just cruel—it's petty.

I paused halfway up the steps, momentarily blinded by the sunlight reflecting off his aviators and the unmistakable glint of smugness that came with being a famous musician in designer boots. His dark hair was artfully tousled like he'd just rolled out of bed with a guitar and a minor chord. His jawline had only gotten sharper, more capable of slicing through steel, silence, or my remaining dignity.

Well. Fantastic.

Behind me, Meg nudged my back with her purse. "Keep it moving, Ari. This isn't the Oscars."

"Oh, I don't know," I murmured. "I see a lot of acting already."

Meg snorted, but I kept my eyes forward. One foot in front of the other, like I was walking toward justice and not the inside of a flying panic attack.

Jeremy was waiting at the top of the steps like a human buffer. "You okay?"

"I'm *great*," I replied, voice dipped in sarcasm. "Really enjoying this new immersive therapy technique. It's called 'Surround Yourself With Everything That Traumatized You and Smile.'"

He winced, the way a brother does when he knows he's stepped on a landmine of his own design. Good. Let him squirm.

I stepped onto the jet and immediately understood why Luke Knightley could casually afford to invite a dozen people to Vegas on a whim. The interior looked like an *Architectural Digest* photo shoot had collided with a luxury whiskey ad and birthed a sky mansion. Cream leather seats, gold accents, and windows that dimmed with a touch.

And at the back of it, lounging like temptation incarnate, was Christopher. Sitting with one long leg stretched out, leather jacket thrown over the back of his chair like it was being held there by the sheer force of his ego.

He didn't need to be here.

He wasn't in the wedding. He wasn't family. He was simply the bassist in the band Luke fronted. But apparently, that made him important enough to tag along on a weekend designed to celebrate my brother and my friend.

Ellie, Luke's girlfriend and Meg's maid of honor, had apologized to me the moment the group text went out.

"I tried," she said. "I swear I tried. I told Luke it would be awkward."

Awkward? It was a psychological booby trap.

But if Christopher didn't come, he'd be the only band member not invited. And Luke was loyal to a fault, especially when it came to his guys. So here we were. Trapped together in a pressurized tube for four hours, pretending this was fine.

Christopher hadn't even had the decency to decline the invite. Which meant, in my professional opinion, he was still a complete jackass.

"Drinks in the back," Luke called, one arm draped casually around Ellie, who was already scrolling through the weekend itinerary on her phone. "We've got champagne, whiskey, and sparkling water for the emotionally repressed."

"That's mine," I muttered, tossing my carry-on into an empty seat with the grace of a woman barely suppressing a full-scale meltdown.

Meg plopped down beside Jeremy. I took the seat directly across from them and immediately pulled out my e-reader like it was a taser. If anyone needed me, I was elbows-deep in a feminist murder mystery and *not* silently cataloging all the ways my ex had managed to look better with age.

Christopher was across the aisle, two rows back. The plane was wide enough that we weren't breathing the same air, but close enough that if I looked up—and I wouldn't—I could probably smell his cologne.

I hated that I noticed.

I hated even more that he hadn't aged badly. If anything, he looked like a more refined version of the heartbreak I used to cry about at two in the morning, curled up on my bedroom floor with Taylor Swift and a family-sized bag of Chips Ahoy. He was leaner now. The boyishness had burned off and left something more solid, more grounded. Like life had hit him and he'd somehow landed upright.

Liam Dashwood and Nick Holt, the other two members of Whiskey Smoke, were flanking him and cracking jokes that sounded like punchlines to sins they hadn't confessed yet. I didn't want to know. I especially didn't want to imagine any of them hooking up with a bridesmaid mid-flight. Which —let's be honest—wasn't off the table.

Speaking of bridesmaids, two of Meg's college friends were perched at the bar in identical rose-pink hoodies that screamed *"BRIDE SQUAD"* in rhinestones. One of them was named Heather. Or Hailey. Possibly both. I hadn't been introduced, but I was already exhausted by them.

Christopher's head tilted slightly. Just enough that our eyes locked for one searing, godforsaken second.

I didn't flinch.

Didn't blink.

Didn't fall apart.

But my grip on the e-reader did tighten like I was one chapter away from murder.

Instead of throwing it, I gave him a nod. Cool. Dismissive. Legal-drama-level lethal.

He raised a hand in response, maybe a wave. Maybe a peace offering. Either way, I blinked once—slowly, like a judgmental owl—and turned back to my book.

Let the record show: I acknowledged him. Briefly.

Further, let the record also show: I hadn't burst into flames. Progress.

Meg leaned over and whispered, "You okay?"

"Peachy," I said without looking up. "And by peachy, I mean currently weighing the pros and cons of emergency exit door access mid-flight. Is there a parachute on board, by chance?"

She gave me a look that hovered somewhere between pity and admiration. "You know you'll have to talk to him eventually."

"Only if I'm legally compelled to."

Jeremy chuckled. "God, I missed this dynamic."

A flight attendant in a crisp black uniform offered me a champagne flute. I took it and raised it in mock salute.

"To old flames," I said. "May they stay where they belong: in the past, and preferably on fire."

Ellie winced.

I straightened my shoulders and stared straight ahead. I wasn't here to have a second chance. I wasn't here to forgive.

I was here to celebrate my brother, support my friend, and maybe—*maybe*—prove to myself that I'd evolved beyond the girl who used to wait by her phone for a call that never came.

No flirting. No reminiscing. No wondering what his lips would taste like now.

Absolutely *no* imagining how that soft black t-shirt would feel bunched in my fists.

Nope. Not happening.

I took another sip of champagne.

Vegas hadn't even started yet.

And I was already burning.

CHAPTER 5

Thursday afternoon — Las Vegas — Christopher

The second I stepped off the jet, the Nevada heat hit me like a sucker punch while Ariana's gaze hit me like a freight train made of ice.

She didn't say a word. Just put on her sunglasses, adjusted her bag strap like it was a weapon, and breezed past me as if I were part of the scenery. Like I was the baggage cart. Or worse—*forgettable.*

Which was rich, considering she was the only thing I've never managed to forget.

Holt slapped my back as we stepped onto the tarmac. I glanced around automatically—habit, after all these years—and sure enough, our security team was already there, stationed discreetly near the edge of the hangar. Black polos, earpieces, and that unmistakable air of calm vigilance. No one had made a scene yet, but it was only a matter of time. Vegas had eyes everywhere. Phones. Paparazzi. Fans who knew what Whiskey Smoke looked like, even in sunglasses.

I caught one of the guards giving me a quick nod—standard check-in. I returned it, then turned back just in time to catch Ariana clocking the whole setup, her jaw tightening ever so slightly. Yeah. She definitely hadn't missed it. She didn't say anything, but I felt her judgment from across the asphalt.

"You good, man?" Holt asked from beside me.

"Yep," I lied.

He gave me a look. "You sure? You're doing that thing."

"What thing?"

"That thing where your face says 'I'm fine' but your soul looks like it's dying a little."

I ignored him. Up ahead, Jeremy and Meg were in deep conversation with the event planner-slash-coordinator-slash-masochist in charge of corralling this entire pre-wedding circus. The bridesmaids were fluttering around in perfectly curated outfits, already taking selfies like we were filming a reality show.

Ariana? She was next to Meg. Her posture screamed politeness and proximity, but her expression was detached, like she might bolt at any second and hitchhike home in a convertible.

She looked *amazing*.

Hair pulled back in a sleek dark ponytail. Oversized sunglasses. Black tank top, high-waisted jeans, little boots that could kick you in the chest if you got too close. She'd always dressed sharp, even back when we were broke and stealing coffee filters from the dorm lounge.

Now she looked like a woman who won court cases for breakfast and burned hearts for fun.

I waited until we were herded into the Sprinter van, waiting to take us to the hotel, before I made my move. She was sitting next to Ellie and one of the bridesmaids—Brittany? Courtney?—scrolling her phone like the screen owed her money.

There was a space across from Ariana. My moment.

I sat down.

"Hey, Ariana."

Her head turned slowly, and she lowered her sunglasses with surgical precision.

"Oh," she said. "You speak."

"Figured I should at some point," I offered with a half-smile.

She nodded. "Well. Don't strain yourself." She gave me a tight smile.

I breathed out a laugh. "Still sharp as ever."

"I'm a prosecutor. I get paid to eviscerate people."

Ellie stifled a laugh. The bridesmaid straight-up gasped.

A beat passed.

"You look good," I said. Because I'm an idiot.

"Thank you," was her only reply.

"Look," I said, trying again, "I didn't think you'd be coming."

Her brow shot up. "That's funny. I'm in the wedding. I'm the *groom's sister*. You, however, didn't need to come."

"Luke invited me. Said it wouldn't be the same without the full band."

"And you couldn't say no?"

"I didn't want to."

Ariana made a show of turning back to her phone. "We don't need to talk. In fact, I'd prefer if we didn't."

The message was clear. The conversation was over.

Holt raised his eyebrows at me from the next seat over. *How's that going?* his look said.

I gave him a look back that translated to *shut up before I write a breakup album with tons of drum solos.*

The rest of the ride passed in uncomfortable silence. At least on my end. Ariana was chatting with Ellie and the bridesmaid, while ignoring me like it was her full-time job. I stared out the window, pretending I wasn't counting the ways I'd already screwed this up.

By the time we reached the hotel—a sprawling, glitter-drenched monument to luxury—I was already mentally halfway through a bottle of bourbon. Nick and Liam made a beeline for the bar in the lobby, and I wasn't far behind.

Bourbon on the rocks. Then another. I didn't speak. Didn't joke. Just sat there and let the alcohol take the edge off the ache that had been sitting in my chest since she turned away.

Ariana was across the lobby, laughing at something Meg said. The sound hit me right in the chest. Not because she laughed—but because it wasn't with me.

Once, it had been with me.

We'd had plans. A future. A messy, wonderful, duct-taped-together kind of life that involved coffee at midnight and arguments about takeout. A shared toothpaste. A cat we rescued during a thunderstorm. Jokes no one else understood.

And I threw it away.

Because I thought I was being noble. Because I thought letting her go would give her the life she deserved.

I didn't want to hold her back. So I let her walk away.

And now?

Now she looked at me like I was a mistake she didn't remember making. A bad decision in retrospect. A song she skipped when it came on the radio.

I downed the last of my drink.

We checked in. Security had to disband a group of fans in the lobby. Room keys were passed around. There was some confusion with the luggage—someone packed a bag full of prank props—but it all blurred together.

In the private elevator, Ariana didn't look at me once. Not when I held the door. Not when I pressed the button for the floor. Not even when she brushed past me when her floor came up.

She stepped out without a word.

And I stood there, watching the doors close between us.

I wasn't drunk.

Not yet.

But I was dangerously close to remembering how good she used to feel in my arms.

And even closer to admitting that no matter how far I'd come...

I'd never really left her behind.

CHAPTER 6

Thursday evening — Ariana

Meg's suite was straight-up ridiculous. I'm talking gold fixtures, plush rugs, and a view of the Vegas Strip that could make a grown woman cry. Two bedrooms. Four bathrooms. A soaking tub that looked like it required a user manual. There was even a minibar stocked with tiny champagne bottles. Because of course there was.

Meg had insisted on booking a suite with private rooms on the same floor for all the bridesmaids. "We're adults, not camp counselors," she'd said, as if that explained the Egyptian cotton sheets and bottle service.

Now, her room looked like a high-end bridal boutique had exploded all over it. Makeup bags littered every flat surface. Curling irons, straighteners, brushes, and a battalion of hair products were scattered around like we were prepping for battle.

And in a way, we were.

"Are you doing okay?" Ellie asked softly, meeting my eyes

in the mirror. She was adjusting her lashes, but she wasn't fooled. Not by me.

After years of avoiding this conversation, I could tell she wasn't letting me dodge it anymore.

I shrugged, reaching for my lipstick. "He's still maddeningly hot. Unfortunately."

Courtney, one of Meg's bridesmaids, let out a delighted snort. "Who? Christopher Wentworth? Girl. That man's a walking billboard for Bad Decisions You'll Never Regret."

I turned and gave her a look. A slow, unimpressed sweep from head to toe. She didn't even flinch.

Bold of her.

Ellie, bless her, stepped in with diplomatic grace. "Christopher and Ariana have…history."

"History?" Haley perked up. "With a face like that, he could break my heart after a one-night stand and I'd still bake him muffins."

I bit the inside of my cheek so hard I might've drawn blood.

Meg's head snapped up. "Courtney, Haley, could you do me a huge favor and grab some ice for the champagne?"

Courtney opened her mouth like she was going to argue, but Haley nudged her. "C'mon, Court. You don't want Meg going full Professor Knightley on us."

Once the door clicked shut behind them, the air shifted. Less suffocating. More…familiar.

Meg turned to me with a wince. "Sorry. They don't know how serious you and Christopher were."

Ellie perched beside me on the bed. "You never really told me what happened, Ari. I mean, I know he broke your heart…but how?"

I should've deflected. Said something breezy and vague. But the truth was sitting there, just beneath my skin. Waiting.

"I'd just finished my last exam. Junior year," I said, voice flat. "He was supposed to pick me up. We were going to drive home for the summer together."

Meg stilled with her brush in midair.

"He showed up with Jeremy. And two guys I didn't know. Movers."

Ellie's eyes widened.

"He broke up with me right there. Outside my dorm room. Said someday I'd see it was for the best."

I could still see the beige cinderblock walls. Still hear the echo in the hallway. I'd stood frozen as they carried out my things—box by box. Not our things. Just mine. But it didn't matter.

Because everything inside me had changed.

"I haven't let anyone in since," I admitted, so quietly I wasn't sure they'd heard. "That was the last time I trusted someone that much."

The room went silent. Just the sound of Vegas humming beyond the windows.

Meg reached for my hand. Ellie squeezed my arm.

No pity. No platitudes.

Just understanding.

Because sometimes heartbreak doesn't show up in fireworks and grand betrayals.

Sometimes it's a quiet goodbye in a beige hallway.

And the kind of scar you learn to live around.

Until Vegas comes calling again.

CHAPTER 7

High school — Christopher

It started in the cafeteria—like most bad decisions and unforgettable moments in high school.

I was halfway through my usual lunch—two peanut butter sandwiches, a bag of chips, and a lukewarm soda—when I spotted her.

Ariana Remington.

She was arguing with the assistant principal about a parking ticket. Her tone was composed, her eyes flinty, her words surgical. She didn't technically have a parking pass. I did—senior lot, space #37. But she was determined to fight the fine on principle.

Even at barely sixteen, Ariana cared about justice. And about being right. Watching her verbally dismantle a school official with nothing but logic and thinly veiled disdain was...well, something else.

She didn't see me at first. Her ponytail was tight, her jaw tighter, and her tray of cafeteria food untouched. I knew who she was—my friend Jeremy's little sister. Sophomore. Honor Society. AP everything. Unofficially terrifying. Officially magnetic.

I waited until the assistant principal retreated in defeat, then slid into the seat across from her and stole a fry off her tray.

"You've got the debate team energy of someone who alphabetizes their arguments," I said.

She blinked. Slowly. "Excuse me?"

"That was an impressive takedown. Ten out of ten. Would not want to face you in a courtroom."

She arched a brow. "You won't. Because I'll be the prosecutor and you'll be the defendant."

I grinned. "See? This is why I sat down."

"Because you have a death wish?"

"Because you're the most interesting person in this cafeteria."

She stared at me. "What do you want, Wentworth?"

I shrugged. "Mostly a milkshake. But also, I figured I'd find out what you're really like."

"You literally practice guitar in our garage twice a week. You've seen me doing laundry and yelling at Jeremy about using all the milk."

"Sure," I said. "But that was before you destroyed an adult with a laminated map of student parking."

A flicker passed across her face. Not quite a smile. But close.

"I'm not supposed to talk to you," she said eventually.

"Why not?"

"You're my brother's friend."

"That's a terrible reason."

"It's the only reason."

"And yet," I said, stealing another fry, "you're still talking to me."

That earned me a sigh. "You're annoying."

"So I've been told."

I reached into my bag and pulled out the chocolate milk I'd grabbed from the vending machine on the way over. I slid it across the table toward her. I'd seen her drink one every day for a week.

She hesitated. Then cracked it open and took a sip.

"Still not talking to you at home," she said.

"Fair. But here? You're kind of stuck with me."

We started talking that day. And the next. And the next.

She was brilliant. Relentless. Opinionated. She wore sarcasm like armor and breathed ambition like oxygen. She didn't giggle or flirt. She challenged. And I kept coming back for more.

I wrote a song about her that week. She told me my chorus needed work.

She was right.

A couple weeks later, I offered her a ride home after band practice. Luke and Jeremy were meeting us for tacos, but I took the long way. The sun was setting. Her ponytail was undone for once, her laugh rare and quiet in the dark.

When I pulled into a side lot behind the taco place, she leaned toward me. Or maybe I leaned toward her. Either way, she kissed me. Quick. Sure. Like it wasn't her first time thinking about it.

She smelled like strawberries and soap.

When we broke apart, she said, "Don't tell Jeremy."

I nodded. "I won't."

Then I went home and wrote another song.

It became a thing. Late-night drives. Study dates that turned into make-out sessions. Me sneaking her into band practice and her offering more brutally accurate lyric edits. We kept it quiet. For a while.

She challenged every assumption I had about what I wanted in a girl. She didn't care about my band. She didn't care that I barely passed geometry. She cared about truth. About justice. About doing things the right way, even when they were hard.

And she made me want to be better.

There was this one day—just a Tuesday. She was in the hallway convincing her AP History teacher to give the class a rewrite on a quiz because it had one unfair question. And I watched her—saw the way she gestured with her hands, the fire in her eyes, the calm fury in her voice—and I knew.

I was done.

She had me.

She was two years younger. Two years smarter. And she had her whole future mapped out in sharp, bold lines.

I didn't know where I was going.

But I wanted her there when I got there.

And I didn't even know I was falling until I was already flat on my back for her.

CHAPTER 8

Thursday evening — Christopher

Our suite was insane. Of course it was.

Three sprawling bedrooms, three marble-and-gold bathrooms, a living room big enough to host a medium-sized wedding, and a view of the Vegas Strip so bright it felt like you could get a tan just by looking out the window. There was a stocked bar that looked like a mob front in a Martin Scorsese film, and enough plush furniture to stage a catalog shoot.

Dashwood claimed the biggest bedroom within thirty seconds of arrival. Not that I cared. I'd slept in the back of vans, on tour bus benches, and once used a guitar case as a pillow during a layover. A bed was a bed. I tossed my duffel onto the second-largest bed, kicked off my boots, and headed back into the main room, where Liam was already cracking open a beer.

He was perched on the arm of the massive sectional, one foot on the coffee table, remote in hand like a king surveying his domain. But his eyes flicked up the second I walked in, and I knew that look. That quiet curiosity wrapped in brotherly concern.

"You gonna tell us what happened?" he asked. Too casual to be casual.

Out of the corner of my eye, I caught Nick—Holt—frantically waving his hands behind me like he was trying to land a plane. *Don't ask. Don't ask.* He might as well have had cue cards.

Too late. I was already unraveling.

"What happened?" I echoed, heading straight for the bar. I dropped my aviators onto the counter with a clatter and poured a generous bourbon. "I fucked up. That's what happened."

Liam blinked. That easy grin of his faltered.

I took a long sip and dropped into one of the velvet armchairs that looked like they belonged to a 1920s speakeasy.

"Ariana and I—we were the real thing. Or I thought we were. We'd been together since high school. All through college. Until I dropped out senior year to give music everything I had. She still supported me. She was incredible that way."

The Vegas lights shimmered through the glass behind me. All that glitz. All that flash. When I was nineteen, this suite would've been my definition of success.

Now it just looked like a reminder of everything I'd lost.

Dash—Liam—spoke up again. "But?"

I exhaled hard. "But two years after I dropped out, I was still waiting tables at night and playing to empty bars. Meanwhile, Ari was heading to law school like she was strapped to a rocket. I couldn't keep asking her to hitch herself to my disaster. I didn't belong in her world anymore."

"Bullshit," Holt muttered, flopping onto the couch.

I shot him a look but didn't argue. I didn't have the energy.

"I thought I was doing the right thing," I said. "Letting her go. Giving her room to find someone stable. Someone who could give her the future she deserved."

"And you've regretted it ever since," Holt said, not unkindly.

"Every goddamn day."

Dash tapped his bottle against the table. "So tell her that. Hell, tell her now. You're not some broke nobody anymore. You're Christopher freaking Wentworth. You're rich. Famous. You could offer her the world."

I laughed, sharp and humorless. "You don't get it. Ari doesn't care about all that. She never did. She didn't want the spotlight. She wanted me. And I gave her the boot. Now she hates me. I mean, full-on, scorched-earth hatred. She's not mad. She's nuclear."

Nick looked thoughtful. "You sure about that?"

"What do you mean?"

He lifted a shoulder. "Just… She looked at you a couple times. When she thought no one was watching."

"Yeah," I muttered. "Probably to wish I would sponta-neously combust."

"Nope," Dash said. "That wasn't anger. That was the kind of look you give someone when you're trying really hard not to remember what it felt like to love them."

The room went quiet for a beat.

"You think I still have a shot?" I asked finally, my voice rougher than I meant.

Nick stood, grabbing a beer from the mini fridge. "You've got a weekend. If that's not a shot, I don't know what is."

I shook my head. "I'd give anything to make it right."

Dash dipped his beer bottle toward me. "Then maybe it's time to stop regretting and start doing."

I stared down at the carpet. Thought about all the songs I'd written about her. All the times I'd imagined what I'd say if I saw her again. The apologies I never gave. The ones she probably didn't even want anymore.

"I still love her," I said. Quiet. Simple. Like it wasn't the truest thing I'd said in years.

Dash leaned back with a sigh. "Then what the hell are you waiting for?"

Good question.

Nick lifted his beer bottle in the air. "The way I see it, this weekend may just be your last chance, Wentworth."

Damn. Maybe he was right. Maybe Vegas wasn't just the end of the line.

Maybe it *was* my last chance to start something again.

And this time? I wouldn't run.

This time, I'd fight for her.

CHAPTER 9

Later that night — Ariana

The Sprinter van smelled like tequila, hairspray, and bad decisions waiting to happen.

Nick was already on his second pregame beer, Liam was DJing from his phone with increasingly questionable 'party anthems,' and someone (Courtney?) had brought a glittery cowboy hat that was making its way down the bridesmaid row like a cursed object in a horror movie.

The driver had done a double-take when the guys climbed aboard—probably trying to figure out if this was a bachelorette party or a *Rolling Stone* cover shoot. The guys were used to the stares, the whispers, the barely-suppressed fangirl squeals. I was still getting used to being next to that kind of spotlight.

Luke was snuggled into a back seat with Ellie. Those two seriously needed to get a room. Oh, wait. I guess they already had one. With a balcony. And probably rose petals.

Meanwhile, I sat wedged between Courtney and a

window, clutching my sparkly purse like it contained the secret to surviving this night. I wished it did.

"You look amazing, by the way," Meg said, eyeing my strappy black cocktail dress with just the right amount of cleavage, leg, and vengeance. "That's not a compliment. It's a warning."

"Noted," I said, scanning the van like an assassin checking exits. And then—there he was. Christopher. Stupidly hot in a dark-blue button-down with the sleeves rolled like he had a personal vendetta against my willpower. His hair was artfully tousled, which I knew damn well meant he'd been anxiously raking his fingers through it for the last hour. Classic Wentworth.

And his eyes? Oh, his traitorous, dark, remember-every-thing eyes?

Locked on me.

I turned to Meg. "Remind me again why I came?"

"To celebrate your brother and *me*, your fabulous future sister-in-law," she said, clinking her glass against mine. "And because your revenge dress deserved a proper stage."

I didn't laugh. Okay, fine, I *barely* didn't laugh.

Across from me, Christopher was still looking. Not talking. Not smirking. Just...watching.

Whatever. Let him look.

I was here to eat overpriced tapas, drink aggressively, and survive the weekend with my soul intact. Not to get drawn back into the Christopher Wentworth Vortex of Poor Life Choices and Emotional Scarring.

The van pulled up to the restaurant—one of those trendy spots where the plates were small and the cocktails were large and everything came with a sprig of something vaguely inedible. We spilled out onto the curb in a glittery herd, all clattering heels and cologne and chaos.

Inside, the waiter tried to split us into two tables. Meg

shut that down with the efficiency of a woman who had color-coded RSVPs and a vision board for this moment.

We crammed ourselves into one long table like a rehearsal dinner sponsored by Instagram.

Christopher ended up next to me. Of course he did.

"Hey," he said under his breath.

I arched a brow. "Is this the part where we pretend we're friends now?"

He grinned, like that was charming. Like *he* was charming.

He gave a quiet laugh. "Can't blame a guy for trying."

"I can. And I do. Frequently."

He looked sideways at me, as if he was amused. "So… anyone special in your life these days?"

I turned to him slowly. "Curious or jealous?"

His laugh was a little shaky. *Good.* "Just making conversation."

I narrowed my eyes. "And you? Breaking hearts on the tour bus? Do the groupies come with a punch card? Buy five, get a sixth free?"

His mouth curved. "Not exactly."

"Just endless variety then?"

"I've never been much for variety," he said, voice quiet but unshakably certain. "One woman's always kind of ruined me for the rest."

I blinked. Oh no. Absolutely not. He did not get to say that with that voice and that face and those goddamn forearms.

"Well," I said briskly, "maybe she'll send you a fruit basket."

He laughed again. A real one this time. "You'd probably send a subpoena."

"You'd deserve it."

"I probably would."

And just like that, the air shifted. Again. Like it always did with him.

But I didn't come here to get caught up in old chemistry.

I came here to drink overpriced wine, deliver devastating one-liners, and make it out of Vegas without losing my mind.

And I was just getting started.

CHAPTER 10

Even later — Christopher

I knew I was in trouble the second Ariana ordered a second round of drinks and looked me dead in the eye while doing it. The whole night, all I could think about was what Nick said to me in the suite earlier. *"The way I see it, this weekend may just be your last chance."*

Was there anyway he was right? An alternate universe in which Ariana might actually give me another chance?

The first thing I did was confirm she was single. Ariana hadn't exactly appreciated the inquiry. Meg hadn't been much friendlier when I cornered her by the bathroom to ask either. Let's just say I survived, but barely.

"Who wants to know?" Meg had said, her eyes narrowed to slits.

"I do," I'd replied.

"Don't even think about it," Meg had replied, shaking her head and rolling her eyes as she strolled off toward the table again.

I'd been forced to text Jeremy for the information.

Me:

Is Ariana seeing anyone?

Remington:

Oh, bro.

Me:

C'mon man, level with me.

Remington:

Not that I know of. But seriously. Don't.

That gave me pause. Of course it did. But looking at Ariana, I knew I couldn't resist. I was going to go for it. Maybe it was the same ego that had me believing I'd had a chance in the music industry. But I'd done it, hadn't I? I'd beaten the odds once. I might just be able to do it again. Somebody famous once said, "You lose 100% percent of the shots you don't take." That was damn right.

"Another cabernet, please. And a bourbon for my neighbor. He's going to need it." Ariana ran her fingers through her long, dark hair and she looked so sexy, I had to bite the inside my cheek. Time had only made her more gorgeous.

The waitress blinked at me, tapping her pen on her order pad.

"I'll take the bourbon," I said quickly, before Ariana could add something mortifying like "Make it a double—he's got regrets."

We were two hours into the night, and I was already two

and a half drinks into what could only be described as a rapidly deteriorating coping strategy.

Ariana was holding court like she owned the place—sharp, funny, ice-cold with me and charming with everyone else. The kind of woman who'd win a bar fight with a look.

I loved her.

God help me, I'd never stopped.

After dinner, the chaos moved to a rooftop bar, where the music was too loud and the drinks came in absurd neon glasses with flaming fruit and bendy straws. Ariana vanished into a knot of bridesmaids and bachelorette chaos. I lost her for ten minutes. Ten agonizing minutes.

Because I was looking for her.

Everywhere.

Nick handed me a tequila shot like he was issuing last rites. "You're staring."

"I'm not staring."

"Staring with your *soul*," Liam added, materializing on my other side like an annoying angel of truth.

I knocked back the tequila. Then I saw her.

Ariana, standing at the edge of the bar—one hip cocked, head thrown back, laughing at something Ellie said, hair tumbling down one shoulder, the strip lights catching in her dark-green eyes.

And suddenly I was twenty again. Sitting in the grass at campus, listening to her explain her plan to become a prosecutor like it was already a fact. She'd had a water bottle in one hand and ambition blazing in her chest.

I'd loved her then too. And like a dumbass, I'd let her go.

She spotted me. Tilted her head. Walked straight over like she hadn't just burned herself into my bloodstream all over again.

"You're staring," she said.

"Not true," I lied.

Her brow lifted. "Yeah, you are. You're staring like you forgot how to blink."

I shrugged. Probably time to admit it. "I might've been."

She laughed, sharp and low. "Careful, Wentworth. You're not as smooth as you think you are."

"I'm not trying to be smooth."

Her smile faded, just slightly. "Then what *are* you trying to be?"

I opened my mouth. Almost said it.

Then someone handed her a glittery shot glass, and she downed it in one gulp. I watched her throat work and swallowed too.

The moment slipped away.

But if I'd answered her question, really answered it, it would've been: *"I'm trying to be the guy you might still love."*

CHAPTER 11

Very late that night — Ariana

There's a certain point in every night out where you stop asking questions. Questions like: "Is this a good idea?" Or: "Do I need to eat something?" Or: "Is that an actual Elvis impersonator or just a guy in sequins with unchecked confidence?"

That point happened somewhere between the second rooftop bar and the daiquiri place that served drinks in souvenir flamingo cups the size of my arm.

I was having a good time.

Correction: I was *deciding* to have a good time. That was important. That was agency.

Was I doing shots with Meg and Ellie? Yes.

Was I dancing with Courtney and Haley? Also yes.

Was Christopher watching me from across the dance floor like he couldn't decide whether to come talk to me or set my world on fire for old time's sake?

Definitely.

I tossed my hair, downed the rest of my drink, and grabbed Ellie's hand as the next song came on.

"Is this the one with the line dance?" I shouted.

"No idea!" she yelled back, laughing.

Perfect.

Someone bumped into me. I spun around. It was him.

Christopher.

Of course.

"Sorry," he said, hand on my elbow like he thought I might topple.

I was not going to topple. My heels were solid, my spine was held up by sheer vengeance, and I had enough tequila in my system to defy physics entirely. I could fly if I wanted to.

"I'm good," I said, brushing him off. "You don't need to rescue me."

"I'm not trying to," he said. "I'm just—"

"You're just *hovering*," I said. "Like a big, sad memory with a perfect jawline."

He blinked. "That's...oddly specific."

"I'm oddly specific," I replied, stabbing a straw into another drink that had appeared in my hand. "You knew that. Once."

His smile was slow. Pained. "I never forgot."

Too much. The music was too loud. The lights were too much. His eyes were *definitely* too much.

"Don't," I said, backing away. "Don't get sentimental on me now, Christopher. That ship has sailed. Crashed. Sank. The band played. Everyone drowned."

"I didn't drown," he said.

"You didn't have to," I snapped. "You left the boat before the storm."

I turned away before he could respond, letting the crowd swallow me back up. I found Meg. I hugged her. I kissed her on the cheek and made her promise not to let me tragic text anyone. She promised.

More drinks. More dancing. Glitter. Screaming laughter. A conga line. A random bachelorette party from Florida that tried to recruit us. I may have stolen one of their veils. No one stopped me.

The night blurred at the edges like a photo with too much flash.

Christopher found me again in a cab line. Or maybe I found him.

"Where are we going?" I asked.

"Wherever you want," he said, a little breathless, like I was the only real thing in the world.

I remember lights. I remember a fake bouquet. I remember someone asking if I wanted "The Elvis Deluxe" or "The Classic Romance Package."

I remember turning to Christopher and saying, "You always were trouble."

And he grinned and said, "You always liked that."

I remember laughing.

And then—

Nothing.

CHAPTER 12

High school — Ariana

I never meant to fall for Christopher Wentworth.

He was the kind of boy you were supposed to avoid in high school. Tall, cocky, always surrounded by a crowd of guys who smelled like Axe and ambition. He played bass guitar in a band that practiced in our garage and left behind empty soda cans and broken strings. He had a smile like a dare and a jawline that made people stupid.

He was also my brother's friend.

Strike one. And two. And three.

I told myself I didn't like him. That he was annoying. Loud. Distracting. He teased me constantly, called me "Remington" like it was a nickname instead of a last name, and stole my fries whenever he sat across from me in the cafeteria. Which, unfortunately, started happening a lot.

He was a senior. I was a sophomore. He had a parking pass and a leather jacket and that look in his eyes like he already knew the world wasn't fair—but he was going to charm it into submission anyway.

And God help me, I liked him for it.

He talked to me like I wasn't just Jeremy's sister. Like I wasn't just the girl in too many AP classes, who knew all the answers and never let anyone copy her notes. He asked questions. Listened when I ranted. Laughed when I got worked up about things that didn't matter to anyone else but me.

He brought me chocolate milk on test days.

He made me feel like I could be fierce and soft at the same time.

And then one day, after band practice, on the way to meet Jeremy and Luke for tacos, he picked me up in his Jeep, turned up the radio, and invited me to tag along like it was no big deal. But somewhere between stoplights and a shared smile, he parked, and I leaned across the console and kissed him—I couldn't wait another second.

"Is that okay?" I asked afterward, a little breathless.

"More than okay," he replied, eyes dark and serious. Then he asked if he could kiss me. I said yes and it was...electric.

For the rest of that year, we were a secret kind of magic. We'd meet behind the bleachers after debate practice, sneak out for milkshakes at the one diner no one else seemed to remember. He wrote me songs; I fine-tuned his lyrics. He said I was brilliant. Intimidating. Way out of his league.

He made me feel like the leading character in a story I didn't know I was allowed to be in.

And the worst part?

He meant every word.

That's the thing people don't understand about Christopher.

Even back then—before the band took off, before the money and the magazine covers and the stage lights—he was real.

He didn't love halfway. He didn't kiss like it was casual. He kissed like it was a promise.

We were young. Stupid. Unstoppable.

Until we weren't.

And now, sometimes, I'll hear a chord or a lyric or that dumb laugh of his from across a hotel bar in Vegas and remember the boy who used to pull me into his lap in the front seat of his Jeep and say, "If I make it, you're coming with me."

And I remember the girl who believed him.

She didn't exist anymore.

But sometimes, I still missed her too.

CHAPTER 13

Thursday night (technically Friday morning) — Christopher

Okay. I admit. I should've stopped it.

That's what kept running through my head.

I should've stopped it. Said no. Laughed it off. Called a car. Taken her back to the hotel and gotten her a bottle of water and a grilled cheese sandwich and let her pass out like a normal drunk person.

But instead—

I married her.

Because when Ariana turned to me in that absurd little wedding chapel, with neon roses and a cardboard cutout of Elvis presiding over the guest book, and said, "Let's do it," I forgot everything that should have made me say no.

And I remembered everything that ever made me say yes to her.

It started with a cab ride, where she held my hand like it was the only steady thing in the universe. We passed a place with twinkle lights and lots of hearts and a hand-painted sign that said "True Love Wedding Chapel," and Ariana pointed and said, "That's hilarious. Let's do it."

I laughed.

She didn't.

"I'm serious," she said. "Let's get married. For the jokes."

"Ari—"

"What? You scared?" she said, tipping her head, hair falling over one shoulder.

Never.

I told the cab driver to pull over.

Inside, it smelled like coconut air freshener and whatever mistakes were made earlier that day. The woman behind the desk wore a tiara and had a tattoo of dice on her wrist. She asked if we wanted Elvis or Traditional.

Ariana looked at me. "You pick. You're the groom."

I forgot how to breathe.

We picked Traditional. There was a silk bouquet and a rhinestone ring and a dude named Kenny with a ponytail, who officiated like he'd done this three hundred times and once for Britney Spears.

"Do you, Christopher Wentworth, take this woman—"

"Yes."

"A little quick there," Kenny muttered.

"I do," I said again, slower, voice catching in my throat.

Ariana looked up at me, eyes bright, smiling like she meant it. Like there was no past. No heartbreak. No hurt. Just me and her and Vegas and whatever fire we still hadn't put out.

"Do you, Ariana Remington—"

"I do," she said, clearly and loudly, like she was winning something.

And maybe she was. Or maybe I was.

We kissed. Someone clapped. I think Nick tried to Face-Time me at one point. We took a selfie with Kenny. They gave us a certificate in a cardboard frame and a pair of heart-shaped sunglasses.

She looked at me as we stepped outside into the warm, buzzing desert night, barefoot now because she'd lost one heel in the cab. Her hand was in mine.

"You always were trouble," she said, slurring a little, eyes glassy.

"You always liked that," I said.

And then she leaned her head on my shoulder.

By the time we got back to the hotel, she was asleep in the cab.

I carried her up to her room. Got the key card out of her purse.

She didn't wake up when I laid her on the bed.

Didn't stir when I pulled the blanket over her or when I set the water bottle and Tylenol on the nightstand.

I sat there in the dim glow of the hotel lamp, staring at the cheap little gold ring on my finger.

I'd married her. A slow smile spread across my face.

She wouldn't remember. But I would.

And I wasn't sure if that made it better. Or worse.

CHAPTER 14

Friday morning — Ariana

The first thing I felt was my head pounding. The second thing I felt was regret. The third thing…was a ring.

On my hand.

I glanced down. A *gold* rhinestone ring?

I blinked, sat up, and immediately regretted both decisions.

The room was spinning gently. My mouth tasted like tequila and bad judgment. I reached for the water bottle on the nightstand like it was a lifeline and chugged half of it before I noticed what was sitting next to it.

A folded piece of paper.

Wait, no.

Not paper.

Cardstock.

My stomach turned before I even opened it.

"TRUE LOVE WEDDING CHAPEL" was printed across

the top in swoopy, delusional font. There were tiny hearts stamped in glitter ink.

My name was on it.

So was his.

Christopher. Wentworth.

Oh. My. God.

I screamed.

I launched the cardstock across the room. It bounced off a chair and fluttered to the floor like a taunt from the universe.

We got married?

A brief image flashed through my mind. An officiant who looked starstruck. He probably thought he was marrying two drunk impersonators until he saw Christopher's real name on the license. Then again, maybe rock stars getting hitched at two a.m. wasn't even that unusual around here.

My thoughts were interrupted when a soft knock came at the door. "Ariana?"

Holy hell. Christopher was out there. And he knew. *He knew*! And he let it happen?

My rage hit DEFCON 1.

"DO NOT SPEAK TO ME THROUGH A DOOR RIGHT NOW, CHRISTOPHER."

Silence.

Then, quietly, "Can I come in?"

"Unless you've brought a time machine or a damn annulment attorney, you better *not*."

The door cracked open anyway. He peeked around it cautiously, as if I might be armed.

I was not. But I was *dangerously* close to throwing the water bottle at his head.

He stepped inside, hands raised. "You're awake."

I sat up straighter—then immediately realized how little I

was wearing. Tank top. Panties. His eyes flicked down, just for a second, before he looked away like a gentleman with a guilty conscience. I stood and yanked my silk robe off the end of the bed, pulled it on, fast and furious, tying the sash so tight that I nearly cut off circulation.

"Yes, I'm awake," I thundered. "And I see I got *married* last night. A miracle, considering I *don't remember a damn thing.*"

He winced. "I was going to tell you."

"When?" I growled. "After the honeymoon? Or maybe at our *first anniversary dinner,* when you surprised me with a slideshow of our vows?"

"I was waiting for you to wake up."

I crossed my arms. "I have one question for you."

He watched me, cautious. "What's that?"

"Were *you* sober?"

He hesitated. "Not…entirely."

"But sober enough to know what we were doing?"

He winced, then nodded. "Yeah. I knew. And I wanted it."

My heart thudded once, hard. Damn him.

"Ari—"

"No," I snapped. "Do *not* call me that right now. You lost nickname privileges somewhere around the point when you LET ME DRUNK-MARRY YOU."

"You said you wanted to," he argued, as if that was even remotely the point. "You looked me in the eye. You said, 'Let's do it.' You were smiling."

"I smile at waiters when they forget my side of fries. That doesn't mean I want to legally bind myself to them!"

He ran a hand through his hair. "I didn't think you'd actually go through with it, and then you did, and I— I don't know. I thought maybe—"

I held up a finger. "No. Do not *maybe* me right now. Do not give me wounded puppy eyes. I don't care if I climbed up on a table and screamed *MARRY ME, CHRISTOPHER, RIGHT NOW OR I'LL FIGHT ELVIS*, it was *your* job to say no."

"But I didn't want to say no."

Oh.

Oh no.

I blinked. "You…what?"

He stepped closer. "I didn't want to say no. I never wanted to say no to you. Not then. Not now."

I took a step back, hands up. "You don't get to make this romantic. You don't get to turn this into some Nora Roberts plot twist. This is *real*, Christopher. You married me without my consent—"

"You were consenting plenty at the time," he said, too fast.

I went still. Dead quiet.

"You want to rephrase that?" I asked, voice cold enough to freeze a volcano.

He blanched. "I mean—you were joking, but also serious, and I didn't— Shit, that came out wrong."

I stalked over and grabbed the fake marriage certificate off the floor, waving it like evidence in a trial. "Well, congratulations. You got what you wanted. But I am filing an annulment *today*."

His jaw tensed. "You don't have to—"

"*Oh*, I do. I'm an attorney, Christopher. I know exactly how fast I can get this overturned. And guess what? *It's gonna be fast*. Like *Guinness Book of World Records* fast."

He looked at me like I'd just punched him. I kind of wanted to.

"You really don't remember anything?" he asked softly.

"No," I said. "And even if I did—I'd still want out."

I stormed past him, into the bathroom, and slammed the door.

I stared at myself in the mirror.

Glitter in my hair. A smudge of mascara. A tiny rhinestone heart sticker stuck to my neck.

And a ring.

Still on my finger.

I yanked it off and set it on the counter like it was poison.

Then I turned on the shower, stepped in, and tried to scrub away the worst mistake I'd never meant to make.

CHAPTER 15

Same time — Christopher

Ariana slammed the bathroom door like she'd just finished a closing argument.

I stood there for a full thirty seconds, letting the echo settle.

Then I looked down at my ring.

It was gold-plated, not real, but somehow it looked like it belonged on my finger. Like fate had a sense of humor and a shopping cart full of clearance accessories.

I could not bring myself to take it off. I didn't want to.

I walked to the window and looked out at the Vegas skyline—glassy towers, fake pyramids, a giant Eiffel Tower pretending nothing was insane.

Somewhere down there was a wedding chapel with two empty champagne flutes, a receipt, and a framed picture of us I never should've let them take. No doubt it would end up on a celebrity gossip website within hours. That was my life now. But I couldn't even get mad about it. Because all I could think was...*I'm married to Ariana. Finally.*

And yeah. Maybe I should've stopped it.

But I hadn't.

Because for one minute—one real, perfect, late-night moment—I let myself believe it was possible. That maybe we could rewrite the ending. That maybe Ariana still felt it too.

She hadn't. Or she didn't remember. Same result either way.

The shower turned on behind the door. My mind helpfully offered a visual. I told it to shut up.

I made myself a cup of hotel coffee and leaned against the desk, waiting.

Ten minutes later, she emerged in a cloud of steam and fury, wrapped in a fluffy white towel, hair dripping, skin flushed. She froze when she saw me still standing there.

"You're still here?" she asked, incredulous.

I took a sip of coffee. "We're married." I couldn't help the grin I gave her.

Her eyes narrowed. "Nope. Annulment, remember? Stat."

"I remember." I set the cup down. "But I'm going to ask you to wait."

She barked a laugh. "Wait? For what? The part where you trick me into a vow renewal?"

I smiled. "Tempting. But no."

She crossed her arms. The towel dipped a little. I noticed. I tried not to. I failed.

"I'm serious," I said, voice low. "Just...wait. Forty-eight hours. That's all I'm asking."

She stared at me like I'd grown a second head. "Two days?" she said. "Of what—honeymooning?"

I stepped closer. Not to intimidate. Just to *be* there. To make her *feel* it.

The pull. The heat. The past that hadn't burned out—just gone underground.

"No expectations," I said. "No pressure. Just...don't file yet. Let's see what happens."

She shook her head. "What happens is that I lose brain cells and you get your little fantasy reunion."

"That's not what this is."

"No?" She tilted her head. "Then tell me what this is, Christopher. Make it make sense."

I looked at her. Really looked at her.

And then I said the thing I'd been holding back since the day I walked away from her.

"I never stopped loving you."

First, she gasped.

Then she blinked. Hard.

I didn't move. Didn't flinch.

I forced my voice to remain calm. "Back then, I thought walking away was the right call. You had this future—a *real* future. And I was some broke kid chasing a dream. I didn't want to be the reason you gave up law school or *any* of it. I thought letting you go was the one good thing I could do."

"You didn't let me go," she snapped, voice rough. "You *dropped* me."

"I know," I said quietly. "And I've regretted it every day since."

Silence stretched between us like a wire ready to snap.

"You're not the only one who remembers everything, Ari," I said. "I remember what it felt like when you laughed at my terrible jokes. I remember the little mole on your hip you used to complain about and I used to kiss. I remember what it was like to wake up next to you and know I was exactly where I was supposed to be."

Her jaw clenched. She looked away.

I took one step closer.

"Give me two days. If you still want to get an annulment after that, I won't stop you. Hell, I'll drive you to the courthouse myself. But for forty-eight hours…let's pretend last night wasn't a mistake."

She didn't answer.

But she didn't say no either.

And that?

That was enough—for now. And I had another card to play.

CHAPTER 16

Two seconds later — Ariana

But the longer I stood there—robe tied, pulse settling—the fury that had carried me this far started to thin out around the edges. I couldn't keep pretending I'd been some clueless victim in all of this. The memories were hazy, but not gone. I'd smiled. I'd laughed. I'd kissed him like I meant it. I'd dragged him into that chapel like it was a dare and said vows like I believed them.

I hadn't been hauled to the altar against my will—I'd marched there, glitter in my hair and tequila in my veins, fully complicit in my own chaos.

But still. He'd been more sober than me. Sober enough to know better.

And right now? That didn't feel romantic. It felt like he should've stopped us—and he didn't.

Why was he even still here? Leaning against the credenza, arms crossed, annoyingly broad shoulders casually eating up space like he belonged there. Like *this* wasn't a total disaster.

I gripped my anger like a shield, because beneath it was

something fragile and stupid and still breathing. Something like hope.

"There's no way I'm waiting," I snapped before he could say anything else insane.

"What if we make a deal?" he asked calmly.

A deal? Good. Perfect. He had no idea who he was dealing with. I was highly trained in the art of negotiation. Law school had taught me the strategy. The DA's office had sharpened it to a blade. Men tried to out-maneuver me in court every single day. And they always left bleeding.

My eyes narrowed even further, which I honestly didn't think was possible. "I don't make deals with people who ambush me at a wedding altar."

He didn't flinch. "I'm only asking for forty-eight hours."

I folded my arms. "To do what exactly?"

"Nothing you don't agree to. No pressure. No games. Just time. Two days."

I rolled my eyes so hard I practically saw heaven. "So I wait, and then what?"

"If you still want an annulment in forty-eight hours..." He paused, straightened. "I'll give it to you. No arguments. No guilt. No passive-aggressive Elvis impersonator commentary."

I opened my mouth to tell him no.

"And," he added, "I'll donate two hundred and fifty thousand dollars to your favorite charity."

I blinked. I *must* have heard him wrong. "You'll what?"

"Quarter of a million," he said, like it was spare change. "To any nonprofit you name."

My brain short-circuited. "Are you serious?"

"As our marriage certificate," he said, deadpan. "You walk away, you get the annulment and the donation. No tricks. No loopholes. Just...give me the time."

I stared at him. Hard. Because it was tempting. Of course it was tempting. But not because of the money.

No. It was because I knew exactly what charity I'd name.

The Guardian ad Litem program at the Legal Aid Society of Milwaukee.

My voice was softer when I said, "You'd give that much for forty-eight hours?"

"Yes," he said without missing a beat. "Whatever charity you choose. Under your name."

I hated him a little in that moment. Because he knew *exactly* where to hit me.

And because it worked.

I'd always been a volunteer. In high school and college. Pets, kids, elderly. I'd volunteered anywhere and everywhere they needed me. These days, I did a lot of pro bono work as well. But the Guardian ad Litem program was my real passion lately.

"I don't trust you," I said, crossing my arms tighter.

"You don't have to," he said. "Just trust the contract I already drafted." He pulled a folded sheet of paper from his back pocket. "I had a feeling you'd want it in writing."

I snatched it from his hand and scanned it. It was short but ironclad. Legal. Legally binding, in fact. Of course there were a few things I wanted to add to it.

"Where did you get this?"

He shrugged. "Let's just say I was busy this morning before you woke up."

I stared at him for a long moment. "You actually think you can change my mind in forty-eight hours?"

"I don't know," he said with maddening confidence. "But I think it's worth a shot."

I scoffed. "If I do this," I said. "And it's a *huge* if. This is charity work. I'd be doing it *for orphans.*"

"I understand. Terribly noble of you." He grinned, but

there was something in his eyes that said he was playing a much longer game.

I glared at him. I wanted to scream. To throw something. Preferably *at* him. Instead, I said, "Fine. I'll take your money. I'll take your time. And then I'm going to take that smug look off your face when I walk away with both."

I wanted to believe I was immune. That he had no chance. But as he turned to go—like he hadn't just dismantled my defenses with a single offer—I realized something horrifying.

He might've won the first round.

And I'd just given him two more.

CHAPTER 17

Later Friday morning — Christopher

There are a lot of things I've done in my life that raised eyebrows. Dropping out of college to chase a dream with nothing but a bass guitar and a borrowed amp. Signing a record deal before I'd figured out how to pay my electric bill. Buying a house with six bedrooms and not a single fork.

But walking into the private brunch room in the hotel restaurant with Ariana at my side and saying, *"Hey, by the way, we got married last night,"* definitely cracked the top five.

Dead. Silence.

Luke's mimosa froze halfway to his mouth.

Liam choked on a strawberry.

Jeremy just…blinked. Twice. Then looked at Ariana like she'd just told him she'd joined a biker gang.

Meg made a noise somewhere between a gasp and a screech and then clamped a hand over her own mouth. "You're *kidding*."

Ariana crossed her arms, stone-faced. "Do I look like we're kidding?"

"You look like you're planning a homicide," Ellie said helpfully.

"She is," I muttered.

"I *was*," Ariana corrected, as she took a seat at the end of the long table and put her napkin in her lap.

I did the same.

Jeremy turned his head to look at us, jaw tight. "Someone explain. Now."

I opened my mouth.

Ariana held up a hand. "I've got it." Then, to the table, "Last night, I was very drunk. Someone"—she didn't even glance at me—"let me wander into a wedding chapel, handed me a fake bouquet, and said, 'Sure, this is a good idea.'"

"It *was* your idea," I said calmly.

"Quiet, groom," she snapped.

Liam snorted into his drink.

Ariana continued, cool as a courtroom. "I woke up this morning with a hangover, a marriage certificate, and a shiny gold ring. I am, unfortunately, now married to this man." She gestured at me like I was the sad country song she thought she'd deleted from her playlist. "Temporarily," she quickly added.

Jeremy went pale. Poor guy looked like he was going to pass out. "You...*what?*"

"We're staying married for forty-eight hours," she said, already bracing for the reactions. "Then we file the annulment. And Wentworth here is going to hand over a quarter of a million dollars to the charity of my choice."

"Oh, damn," Liam said, clearly delighted.

I nodded. "If I can't make her agree to give us a try, I lose. She files, I walk. No arguments."

"And," Ariana added through gritted teeth, "he donates $250,000 to the Guardian ad Litem program."

"That's sounds a lot like how I convinced Ellie to be my nurse last summer," Luke interjected.

I scratched the back of my neck. "Yeah, that's kinda where I got the idea."

Ariana rolled her eyes.

"Careful, Ariana, I ended up falling for Luke," Ellie added, wincing.

"Yeah, well, that's not gonna happen here," Ariana said, pointing back and forth between us.

Nick whistled low. "Holy shit. This *is* going to be interesting."

"We've already signed the contract," Ariana continued. "Witnessed by a notary at the front desk."

Meg raised her hand. She was staring at me. "Wait. Christopher, you said you wanted her to give you a try. Does that mean you *want* Ariana to stay married to you?"

"Exactly," I said. "I made a huge mistake breaking up with Ariana years ago. This is the only chance I'll ever have to fix it."

Courtney and Haley, or whatever the bridesmaids were named, made long *awwwwww* sounds while Ariana glared at them.

Jeremy looked between us like we'd both joined a cult.

"Let me get this straight," he said to his sister. "You two have been legally married for less than twelve hours, and now you're entering a forty-eight-hour emotional hostage situation *in Vegas* to see if he can convince you to stay married to him?"

"Yes," I said.

"No," Ariana said at the same time.

We glared at each other.

Liam stood and raised his mimosa. "To Mr. and Mrs. Hot Mess. May your trauma be our entertainment."

The whole table toasted.

Ariana did not.

She just turned to me, eyes blazing. "Forty-seven hours and fifty-five minutes." The countdown started right after the contract had been signed. I'd negotiated for that at the front desk.

And then Ariana picked up her empty plate and walked toward the huge buffet along the side of the room like the damn queen of controlled rage.

I watched her go, a smile tugging at the corner of my mouth.

Let the games begin.

CHAPTER 18

Early Friday afternoon — Ariana

It started with a buzz. Then another. Then a full-on avalanche of vibration from my phone, which was buried under a beach towel and sunscreen in the over-sized tote I'd brought to the hotel pool. They'd given us the VIP section. Again. Turns out, when you vacation with a rock band, velvet ropes just sort of…part.

I almost ignored it. I was sitting on a chaise lounge under a giant umbrella, wearing sunglasses the size of satellite dishes, and trying to pretend I was on vacation and not in the middle of a legal disaster that involved way-too-hot abs.

But the buzzing wouldn't stop.

With a sigh, I reached into the tote, dug around past a slightly crushed granola bar, and pulled out my phone. Twenty-seven missed notifications. Mostly texts. A few emails. One from my boss.

My stomach dropped.

I opened the most recent one. It was from Jillian, another assistant DA in Milwaukee. All it said was:

WTF, Ariana?? Call me.

That was not the kind of message you ever wanted from a colleague. I scrolled up.

My mom just sent me this.

She'd attached a screenshot.

It was from *TMZ*.

The headline screamed in bold, unholy font:

"WHISKEY SMOKE'S BASSIST WEDS BADASS PROSECUTOR IN LATE-NIGHT VEGAS SHOCKER"

Below it, a photo. Of me. Of *me*. Holding a bouquet of cheap, fake flowers and what looked like a rhinestone tiara, standing next to Christopher in front of a neon heart that said "TRUE LOVE WEDDING CHAPEL."

The caption underneath:

"Christopher Wentworth, of Whiskey Smoke, tied the knot with former high school sweetheart and current Milwaukee assistant district attorney Ariana Remington in a surprise late-night ceremony Thursday. No comment yet from either party."

I blinked at the screen, trying to decide if I should throw it or just scream into a pillow.

It got worse.

In addition to my job title, the article named the most high-profile case I'd worked last year.

"Remington, who made headlines in 2024 for prosecuting the Eastside gang conspiracy case, is a rising star in the DA's office."

I dropped the phone like it was radioactive. How the hell did they know all of this?

"Oh no," I whispered.

"What happened?" Meg asked from the next chair over.

She was sipping something pink through a straw and scrolling Pinterest wedding boards.

I held up the phone.

She took one look and gasped. "Oh shit."

Ellie leaned over. "Oh my God. Is that real?"

"It's real. It's very real. And it's everywhere."

My email pinged again. This time from our press liaison at the DA's office.

"Please advise ASAP whether you wish to issue a formal statement or remain silent at this time. Are you available for a call?"

"Kill me now," I muttered.

Meg sat up straighter. "How the hell did they get pictures?"

"There was a photographer at the chapel. I think his name was Kenny. Or maybe Kenny was the officiant. I don't know. I was drunk and emotionally compromised."

Ellie was reading the article on her phone. "Oh no. They have a quote from the chapel manager. She says, 'They were laughing and kissing and seemed totally in love. It was super romantic.'"

"I *will* sue her," I said, standing up and pacing the tile. "I will sue the chapel. I will sue the internet. I will sue Nevada."

Meg grabbed my wrist. "Ari, breathe."

"I'm a public servant," I snapped. "I prosecute dangerous people for a living. I can't be out here looking like I just drunkenly eloped with a rock star in full view of half the internet."

Christopher appeared before I could spiral further. Shirtless. Smirking. Holding a bottle of sparkling water and looking vaguely like a Greek statue but with better hair.

"Hey," he said. "Why is everyone staring at their phones like someone died?"

I whirled on him. "Because *someone* leaked photos of our wedding to *TMZ* and now it's viral, and my *office* wants a statement, and my entire prosecutorial integrity is hanging by a thread!"

His smirk vanished.

He held out the bottle. "Sparkling water?"

I took it without a word and cracked the cap like it was a neck I wanted to snap.

"You don't seem surprised," I said, narrowing my eyes.

"Because I was expecting it," he said. "We were in a public chapel. I recognized one of the staff as a freelance stringer for celebrity gossip sites. I figured it was only a matter of time."

"*You knew?*"

He shrugged. "Suspected. I mean, I've heard those gossip sites keep an eye on Vegas wedding licenses. It was only a matter of time."

I stared at him like he was an alien. "You *wanted* this to go public?"

"No," he said quickly. "I just wasn't trying to hide it."

"Well, congratulations. We're now the punchline of the week, and I'm probably going to get pulled off a case or suspended."

"Suspended? Ari, come on. You didn't break the law."

"I married you while drunk in Las Vegas. That's not illegal, but it's not a good look for a woman whose entire job hinges on credibility."

Ellie stood up. "Do you want me to go get your laptop? You could write a statement. Maybe something neutral?"

Meg added, "Or lean into it. Say it was a personal mistake and you're taking appropriate steps to rectify it. That's kind of the truth, right?"

I sat down, heart racing. I'd spent years crafting my

image. Being taken seriously. Rising through the ranks of the DA's office, even when the old boys' club tried to keep me out. I couldn't afford this kind of attention. Not like *this*.

Christopher knelt next to my chair. "I didn't think it would blow up this fast. But look, I have a plan."

"Oh, this should be rich."

He crouched beside my chair. "We do nothing."

I blinked. "We what now?"

"We don't issue a statement. Not yet. We don't confirm, don't deny. Just let it simmer."

I glared at him. "That's your plan?"

"For now, yeah. Think about it: we've got forty-eight hours under our agreement. If we stay married, there's no scandal. No joke. Just a happy couple—"

I closed my eyes briefly. "Don't say it."

"In love," he finished, grinning like a lunatic.

I narrowed my eyes at him. "You are *deranged*."

"But I'm right," he said calmly. "If we issue something now, it becomes a circus. We say nothing, let it breathe, and if we end up staying married, it retroactively becomes romantic instead of reckless."

"And if we *don't* stay married?" I set down the water bottle and crossed my arms over my chest.

"Then we issue something clean and pre-approved. But later. Not mid-frenzy."

Meg slowly nodded. "He's not wrong. The story only explodes more if you jump in now. People move on fast unless you give them a reason not to."

I sat back, exhaling hard. It made me nuts, but they had a point. "Fine. We only issue a vague placeholder statement for now for now. But we *do* prepare a more formal statement. For when the clock runs out. I want it drafted, vetted, and ready to go the second the forty-eight hours are up."

"Done," Christopher said, way too cheerfully for a man partially responsible for my public unraveling. He turned on his heel, already texting someone—his PR team, probably. Or maybe one of his idiot bandmates, who I was strongly considering billing by the hour for emotional damages.

Meg handed me her iPad. "Just in case. You might want to start sketching the version where you survive this with your dignity intact."

I took it with a sigh.

By the time Christopher's team had their placeholder statement up, the article had already spun off into three TikTok theories, a Reddit AMA from someone claiming to have seen us at the chapel, and at least one Instagram meme featuring my tiara and the words *"BADASS ENERGY"* in Comic Sans.

The official post was short and vague:

"In a private moment that turned unexpectedly public, Christopher Wentworth and Ariana Remington participated in a spur-of-the-moment wedding ceremony. It was a personal decision made during a celebratory trip with close friends. No further details will be shared at this time. We ask for privacy and respect for the couple."

It wasn't terrible. It wasn't great. But it bought us time.

My phone finally stopped pinging. My boss emailed:

"Thanks for the clarification. Let me know if the situation escalates. Otherwise, we'll hold off on a public statement."

Relief washed over me.

Christopher texted:

Crisis (mostly) averted.

I didn't answer.

But I didn't block him either.

Which was probably a mistake.

Or maybe something else.

Because beneath all the outrage and spin control, something quieter had started to settle in.

Something dangerously close to curiosity.

Forty hours to go.

And suddenly, they didn't feel long enough.

CHAPTER 19

Later Friday afternoon — Christopher

One by one, the group scattered. Meg dragged Jeremy off to a couples massage. Nick and Liam left on what they claimed was a "taco run," but sounded more like a dare than a meal. Luke disappeared toward the lazy river, and Ellie was FaceTiming her grandma back in Milwaukee from a shaded cabana like it was a perfectly normal thing to do while surrounded by people in sequins and swim trunks.

The bridesmaids? Flirting shamelessly with a pair of sunburned guys from Michigan over by the non-VIP swim-up bar.

Which left Ariana.

And me.

Alone.

By the pool.

She hadn't said much since the *TMZ* situation went nuclear, but she hadn't stormed off either. And after everything, she'd agreed to the placeholder statement. Nothing flashy. Nothing official. But a pause. A window. A maybe.

To her, it was probably damage control.

To me? It felt like hope disguised as strategy.

Maybe I was delusional, just like she kept insisting. But that tiny concession—the agreement to wait, to breathe, to not burn it all down immediately—felt like something more than just crisis management.

It felt like a crack in the door.

Which meant I needed to step up my game. I only had hours to convince Ariana to give me a real shot, after all.

She was floating on one of those resort loungers that sit half-submerged in the water, sunglasses on, arms stretched behind her like a queen exiling all bad vibes from her kingdom.

I'd never seen her look so relaxed.

Or so absolutely untouchable.

I sat on the pool's edge, feet dangling in, sipping the last of my beer. I wasn't trying to stare at her legs. Or her collarbone. Or the little smile she got when she thought no one was watching.

But I was.

Because even now—*especially* now—Ariana Remington wrecked me.

She opened one eye. "If you're going to stare, at least have the decency to do it without the creeper half-smile."

I grinned. "You always said my half-smile was hot."

"That was *before* you accidentally became my husband."

"Still hot though."

She groaned and pushed her sunglasses to the top of her head. "Do you ever stop?"

"Not when I'm winning."

"You are not winning."

I leaned back on my elbows, warm sun on my skin. "You sure about that? I swear I saw you laugh at something I said earlier."

"I didn't."

"You flinched. With joy."

She rolled her eyes. "Your delusion is truly exhausting."

"I'm persistent. There's a difference."

She floated closer, the gentle motion of the water pulling her near my knees. Inches from me now.

Close enough to smell the citrus in her sunscreen. Close enough to see the way her lashes curled slightly at the ends.

Close enough to remember exactly how it felt to kiss her. To trace my fingertip along the path of the freckles on her nose.

And I wanted to. God, I wanted to.

But I didn't.

Because I wanted it to mean something again—not just be a byproduct of nostalgia and chlorinated chemistry.

She looked at me then, eyes shaded but sharp. "What are you doing?"

"What do you mean?"

"That look."

I shrugged. "Just remembering things."

She snorted. "Well don't. Nostalgia's a trap. Like MLMs. Or pineapple on pizza."

"You used to like pineapple on pizza."

"I also used to like *you*."

Oof. That one should've hurt more than it did. But the heat in her cheeks said otherwise.

"I still like you," I said softly.

That shut her up. Her eyes flicked to my mouth. And for a second—a *single, electric, eternity-long* second—I thought she might kiss me.

Or let me kiss her.

We were close enough. The air between us buzzed with it.

She shifted on the lounger, just slightly, toward me.

I held still.

Waited.

Don't push it, Wentworth. Don't screw it up.

Her eyes dropped to my mouth again.

I forced myself to lean back on my palms, searching for a new subject. Oh, I had one all right. "You ever get serious with anyone else?"

She tipped her head. Eyeing me. I thought for a second she wasn't going to answer. "There've been a couple of guys."

"Oh, yeah? Like who?"

She just smiled. A dangerous, smug little smile. "Wouldn't you like to know."

"I would, actually."

"Yeah, well. Too bad," she said, her voice sharp.

"But you're single now, right?" I pressed.

That got me a laugh. A real one. Loud, bright, and soaked with sarcasm. "Uh, a little too late to ask, don't you think?"

I grinned. "Just want to know who my competition is."

"What about you?" she asked, tossing it out so casually it almost hid the sharp edge beneath. "Any favorite groupies?"

The question hit harder than it should have. I leaned back, squinting at her. "No. A few dates here and there. Nothing serious. And no groupies. That's Liam's thing."

Her lips curved into a smirk. "Big surprise."

I held her gaze, let the grin fade. "I was serious last night. No one ever measured up to you, Ariana."

Her breath caught. Just a tiny hitch—but I caught it. She covered it fast with an exaggerated sigh, waving me off like I was nothing more than a persistent memory. But I wasn't blind. Or stupid.

"You should get Courtney's number," she said airily. "I'm pretty sure she'd stay married to you after the forty-eight hours are up. You might want to trick her into marriage next."

"Not interested." The words came out low, definite. I didn't let Ariana deflect. Not this time.

She tilted her head, studying me. "No?"

"No." I didn't look away. Couldn't. "Only got eyes for you, Ari."

That stopped her. Really stopped her. She didn't have a quip ready. No snark. Just a long, loaded silence while the air stretched thin between us.

God, I wished she knew. Wished she could see herself the way I saw her right now. All sun-drenched and stubborn, trying so hard to keep those walls up while they cracked around the edges.

I wasn't trying to win an argument. This wasn't some game of who could out-snark who. I just wanted her to see it. See me.

And for a second, I think she did.

Her shoulders softened. Her mouth parted, like maybe—maybe—she was going to say something real.

But then she sat up fast, breaking the moment like it never existed. "God, it's hot out here. I need another drink."

She grabbed her towel and headed into the hotel, not looking back.

I watched her go, my chest tightening in that familiar, stupid way it always did around her. And still, despite every-thing, a slow smile pulled at my lips.

Because she'd almost said something. And she'd almost kissed me.

Almost.

And that small, impossible almost? That was enough to

keep me chasing her. Enough to make me believe the next time wouldn't be almost.

It would be everything.

And I wasn't going anywhere.

Not this time.

CHAPTER 20

Friday night — Ariana

I needed a drink.

Not because I was thirsty. Because I was *in danger.*

I nearly kissed Christopher. And what's worse? I *wanted to.*

For about three seconds out there in the pool, the world went soft at the edges. It was just him—tan, shirtless, looking at me like he used to. Like I was the only thing he ever wrote a song about.

I hated that look.

Because I remembered what it felt like when it went away.

Now, back in my room, I was pacing like I was waiting for a jury to return with a verdict. Hair still damp, heart still loud, pacing between the minibar and the absurd gold-accented hotel couch like I was trying to prepare for oral arguments in the case of *Remington v. Emotional Recklessness.*

I was waiting for Meg and Ellie to come to my room. I'd texted them "911" five minutes ago.

I finally stopped pacing, cracked open the minibar, and made myself a vodka soda like it was an emergency.

Which, honestly, it was.

Because I'd almost kissed Christopher Wentworth at the pool!

Voluntarily.

Sanely.

In broad daylight.

I emptied the tiny bottle into a glass and then took a very undignified gulp.

"Ariana Remington," came a voice. It was Meg. I hurried over to the door and let her and Ellie in, glancing down the hallway as if I thought Christopher might just be lurking out there. He was not, but I shut the door quickly anyway.

Meg's sunglasses perched on top of her head, hair still damp from whatever she and Jeremy had been doing at the spa. "We just saw you storm in here like you were about to file a restraining order. What happened?"

"I didn't storm."

Ellie appeared on my other side, settling into the trio like it was a strategy meeting. "You definitely stormed. Jeremy called it a 'classic Ari stomp.' What's going on?"

I glared into my drink. "Nothing."

Meg narrowed her eyes. "Nothing is the most suspicious word in the English language. Spill it."

I swirled the straw and stalled for time.

And then I cracked.

"I nearly kissed him."

The world stopped. I swear, even the TV gave me a moment of silence.

Meg gasped like I'd confessed to treason. "WHAT?"

I set down my drink and covered my face with both hands. "Oh my God. This is why I don't drink during the day."

"You—you almost kissed him?" Meg leaned in like she was trying to keep me from jumping off a ledge. "Like, actually *kissed* him? At the pool?"

"It was a lapse in judgment. A heatstroke situation. Sun poisoning. I don't know. I'm horrified."

Ellie, in true lovable Ellie fashion, shrugged. "If you want to kiss him, kiss him. What's the big deal?"

Meg and I turned to her simultaneously. "No, no, no," Meg said, waving her hands. "That is not the speech we need right now."

"Correct," I said. "I need the 'don't do it, don't even think about it' speech. Fear tactics. Cautionary tales. Consequences."

Ellie just smiled. Smug. Wise. Dangerous. "I spent far too long fighting my attraction to Luke last summer," she said, casually taking a sip from her water bottle. "All it did was make me miserable. And tired."

Meg's mouth opened, closed, recalibrated. "That's not helping."

Ellie shrugged again. "You want me to lie? Tell you to repress your feelings? Give you a PowerPoint on why emotional constipation is fun? Sorry, wrong friend group."

I pointed my finger. "This is unhelpful."

"But is it wrong?" Ellie countered, cocking an eyebrow.

I opened my mouth with a scathing retort primed and ready. But nothing came out.

Because, unfortunately, it wasn't wrong.

"I'll never stop fighting my attraction to Christopher," I said, trying to sound casual. Like that wasn't the most depressing truth I'd ever admitted aloud.

Ellie didn't flinch. "Exactly. Which means you admit that you're attracted to him."

Meg made a tiny wounded sound, clutching her imaginary pearls.

But Ellie's words hit their target. Bullseye. Right in the chest.

"Oh, shit."

There it was.

Not the casual kind of attraction. Not the "oh, he's hot" sort of thing you feel for an unattainable celebrity or a stranger at a bar.

No. This was *Christopher Wentworth*.

The boy who wrecked me. The man who was still doing it.

And I still wanted him.

I dramatically slapped a hand against my forehead.

Meg patted my back with sisterly care. "It's okay, Ari. We'll get through this."

Ellie just batted her eyelashes. "Yeah. Probably by *kissing him*."

I groaned into the bar.

It was already out there—pictures, headlines, hashtags. I couldn't undo that. But maybe the real risk wasn't the press. Maybe it was him. And me.

God help me.

This weekend was going to kill me.

My phone buzzed in my bag, screen lighting up with a new text.

Scott (DA's Office):

You're married? 😳

Attached: a screenshot of the *TMZ* headline.

I groaned and fired back:

It's sooo complicated.

Then I dropped the phone like it burned and let the scream rip free.

Because how the hell had I not taken Scott up on that drink offer?

Because I could've been on a perfectly normal date with a sweet, emotionally available prosecutor who had never done me wrong.

And instead?

I was somehow *married* to Christopher Wentworth.

CHAPTER 21

Twenty minutes later — Christopher

"Everything okay in there?" came Christopher's voice from the hallway.

Meg and Ellie had left, and I was still agonizing over what Ellie had said. Now Christopher was at my door.

"Peachy," I called back. One thing was certain. I needed to stop drinking alcohol. No good could come from it. I grabbed a cherry soda and cracked it open with the kind of focus usually reserved for disarming bombs.

"Are you pacing?"

I immediately stopped pacing. "No."

"Are you sure?"

I opened the door with a stare sharp enough to pierce Kevlar. "I got a drink from the minibar. You want to make that a federal offense too?"

He raised his hands. "Just making sure you're okay."

"Why wouldn't I be okay?"

"Because you almost kissed me earlier."

"What?" I turned immediately so he couldn't see my face go red. He followed me into the room and the door shut behind him.

I perched on the edge of the ridiculous pink-and-gold couch and took a long sip of my cola. He sat on the opposite end, relaxed, infuriatingly confident, legs stretched out like he had all the time in the world and knew I'd break first.

"So..." he said casually, "do you want to talk about earlier?"

I glared at him. "There is no earlier."

His brows lifted. "I'm pretty sure I was there."

I leaned forward. "Let me explain how this works. I float too close in the pool, you get some eye contact, maybe a shared moment of nostalgia and—poof—suddenly you think we're about to rekindle some destiny-fueled romance."

"I mean...yeah," he said with a shrug.

"Look," I growled, "just because you looked *vaguely charming* doesn't mean I was going to kiss you."

His grin deepened. "Vaguely charming. That's the nicest thing you've said to me in a decade."

"I was being *generous*."

"So generous," he said, nodding solemnly. "The humanitarian work continues."

I rolled my eyes, took another sip, and pointed my nose in the air. "It meant nothing."

"Sure," he said, leaning back like he was trying not to smirk. "Totally meaningless. That's why you practically climbed out of the pool like you'd just touched an electric fence."

"I didn't want to get sunburned."

He tilted his head. "Right. Nothing says 'I'm emotionally unaffected' like a full-body sprint away from a kiss that didn't happen."

That was it. I was going to throw something.

My soda. The room key. Possibly myself off the balcony.

"Just admit it," he said, voice suddenly quiet. "It *did* mean something. And it scared you."

I went still.

His eyes were on mine now, serious. Steady.

Too honest. Too knowing.

"I'm not scared," I said.

"Then prove it."

I narrowed my eyes. "How?"

"Have dinner with me tonight. Just us."

A slow, skeptical blink. "Like a date?"

"Like a married couple who can't avoid each other for another twenty-four hours," he said. "And who could both use a meal and a ceasefire."

I wanted to say no.

I *should've* said no.

But my mouth said, "Fine. One dinner. That's it."

He smiled like he'd just won a game I didn't even know I was playing.

"It still meant nothing," I added.

"Sure," he said, as he stood and walked to the door. "That's why you're still talking about it."

He didn't look back.

And I was already losing.

CHAPTER 22

Friday night — Christopher

I f I'd known all it would take to get Ariana to agree to dinner was a poolside near-kiss and a quarter-million-dollar pledge, I would've tried it years ago. Worth every cent.

Getting out of bar-hopping with the others had taken groveling on my part—Remington's eyebrows had nearly shot off his face—but Meg had simply said, "It's up to Ariana." That had been the longest ten seconds of my life.

I'd wanted our wedding to mean something. Instead, it got turned into memes and gossip site fodder. Ariana deserved better than that. I had to make sure she got it. Tonight was my chance.

I'd been holding my breath without realizing it until she walked into the restaurant, five minutes late and somehow still managing to turn every head in the room.

A fan had just asked for an autograph, and I could see the flicker of discomfort in Ariana's eyes as she glanced around, taking in the stares. She had never loved the spotlight—it wasn't her style. She liked control, quiet, knowing who she was without a thousand strangers weighing in. I didn't always love the fame either, but it came with the job. The life I chose. And part of me wondered whether I could truly convince her that we could still make something real inside all the noise.

The second I saw her, it felt like the wind was punched out of me. That dress—deep green, silky, wrapped around her like it had been commissioned by my worst and best dreams. The click of her heels was the countdown to my own destruction. The look in her eyes? A hard, gleaming *Don't get cute.*

God, I'd missed her.

"Nice place," she said, sliding into the deep booth across from me. "I was expecting neon, sequins, and at least one Elvis impersonator."

"Saving that for dessert," I offered. "He sings Sinatra."

Not even a smile. But her mouth twitched. Small victory. I'd take it.

We ordered steaks, wine for her, bourbon for me. The steakhouse was romantic in that expensive, dimly lit way that made her suspicious. Good. Suspicion was better than indifference.

"You picked this place on purpose," she accused, swirling her wine. "Trying to soften me up with ambiance?"

"No. Trying to feed you so you don't murder me." Honest.

"Smart," she said.

We both knew she turned into a Tasmanian devil when she was hangry. She stared at me, long and assessing. I could see her cataloging every move, every breath, measuring how much trouble I was worth.

For a while, we ate in silence. Not uncomfortable. Not comfortable. A truce of sorts. But it couldn't hold.

"I was going to move to LA for you, you know," she said.

The words were soft. But they detonated inside me. My fork stopped mid-air. "What?"

"In college. Junior year. You said you'd probably end up in LA. I started looking at law schools in California."

She'd never told me that. And now, that omission felt like a knife between my ribs.

"You never told me."

"I never got the chance. You broke up with me three weeks later."

God. My throat closed around the burn of alcohol. "I didn't want you to give up your dream. Being a prosecutor in Milwaukee—that was your north star. You talked about it all the time."

"I also talked about you all the time," she said, each word a scalpel, precise and deadly.

I knew. I knew. I had been oxygen to her once. And I'd cut off her air supply without warning.

"You made that decision for me, Christopher. You didn't ask. You assumed. You left."

My insides twisted. "I thought I was doing the right thing."

"You weren't."

"I know that now." The vise tightened. Regret, heavy and suffocating. I'd been a coward. A noble, self-righteous coward.

Her gaze pinned me. "So now what? We just pretend none of that happened?"

"No," I said, voice low. "We let it sit there between us. And then we see if there's anything left."

Her eyes flicked to her wine, then back to me. The wall around her heart was thick. I'd built it there myself.

"This isn't a fair fight," she murmured, her eyes softening just a bit.

"I'm not trying to fight you, Ari."

"Maybe not, but you are trying to win."

I smiled, slow and aching. "Win *you*."

She didn't answer. But the muscle in her jaw betrayed her. Her nostrils flared.

"You're not going to kiss me tonight," she said, and it wasn't a question.

I arched a brow. "Was I going to?"

"You were thinking about it."

Of course I was. Every second. Still was. But she was right. It was too soon. We weren't ready for another collision.

"Not tonight," I said. "Tonight we eat. We talk. We survive each other."

She smirked, but it didn't reach her eyes. "That's what you think."

I should've left it there. But no, I had to push my luck.

"Let's get our own suite. One night. One bed. Zero touching. Just…coexist. Like a science experiment."

Her stare was sharp enough to cut diamonds. "You're proposing proximity as a strategic advantage?"

I grinned. "I'm proposing you'll crack first."

Ariana leaned in, chin propped on her hand. "I'm proposing you're delusional."

"You would've said that about our marriage two days ago. And yet." I spread my hands.

She narrowed her eyes on me. "One bed. No touching. No flirting."

"Scout's honor."

"You were never a scout."

"True. But I'm willing to learn."

We clinked glasses.

And I smiled because tonight, she was here. Sitting across from me. Choosing to stay.

Tomorrow? Tomorrow that bed wouldn't know what hit it.

Later Friday night — Ariana

The suite was too nice. That was my first mistake.

I should've known the second we checked in. The front desk clerk had stammered through our reservation like she was trying not to faint. Apparently, dating a rock star—even accidentally—meant you got penthouses with your room key.

This one had high ceilings and a view of the Strip that shimmered like a glitter bomb went off. The king-sized bed was so cloudlike, it looked like a hotel ad come to life. And the kicker?

Only one of them.

Which I knew going in. I agreed to it.

Because I don't flinch. I don't bend.

And I certainly don't fall for Christopher Wentworth just because he upgraded us to a huge hotel suite with blackout curtains and a bathtub the size of a Manhattan studio apartment.

He dropped his bag by the closet. I dropped mine by the door. We moved like competitors entering a chess match.

"Which side do you want?" he asked, already taking off his jacket.

"Left," I said instantly.

He nodded. "Power side."

I narrowed my eyes. "Don't start with your psychological warfare."

"Noted," he said, heading to the minibar. "Want anything? Whiskey? Water? Self-control?"

I arched a brow. "Oh, I've got plenty of that."

He smiled like that was a compliment.

I sat on the edge of the bed, resisting the urge to sprawl.

He handed me a bottle of water and grabbed one for himself, then stretched out across the right side of the bed like he belonged there.

"Remember," I said, sipping slowly, "no touching. No flirting. No *heat of the moment backsliding into memory lane bullshit.*"

"Crystal clear."

We clicked on the TV. Some vintage crime documentary was playing—low volume, moody narration, and the soft glow of the Strip in the background casting gold across the walls.

For fifteen minutes, we didn't speak.

It was…infuriatingly pleasant.

Then he laughed—low and under his breath—at something the narrator said.

"What?" I asked.

He shook his head. "Nothing. Just reminded me of you."

"Why? Was it the part where the killer used precision and icy detachment to lure his victims into false security?"

"Exactly."

I side-eyed him. "Do not flirt with me using serial killer analogies."

"I wasn't," he said, smile tugging at his mouth. "I was complimenting your ruthlessness."

I bit the inside of my cheek to keep from smiling.

He caught it anyway.

"You're slipping," he said.

"No. I'm tolerant. Big difference."

We went quiet again. I turned onto my side, facing away from him, and clicked the volume up one notch. Focus. Reclaim the moment.

First, his cologne hit me—clean, sharp, devastating. It should've come with a warning label.

Then I felt it.

The heat of him. Just a few inches away. That stupid, solid, reliable presence I used to fall asleep next to for three straight years.

And my body *remembered.*

It wasn't fair. It had no loyalty.

It remembered the way he used to wrap his arm around my waist before we fell asleep. The way his breath would catch when I shifted toward him. The way I never once woke up and didn't feel safe.

I adjusted the covers, trying to push back the memories.

"Still breathing over there?" he murmured into the dark.

"Unfortunately."

He laughed. "This was a good idea."

"No," I said. "This is a *trap.* You're trying to nostalgia me into giving you a second chance."

"Is it working?"

"No."

It was.

I squeezed my eyes shut. "This doesn't change anything,

Christopher. Tomorrow, we go back to normal. You're the guy I used to love. The guy who left."

"And you're the woman who used to love me," he said softly.

I didn't respond.

Because I didn't trust my voice.

And because I didn't want to admit that part of me—some traitorous, flickering part—still might.

CHAPTER 24

Saturday — 1:17 AM — Christopher

I couldn't sleep.

Not with her this close.

Not with the sound of her breathing—slow, even, maddeningly peaceful—curled around my brain like a memory I hadn't earned the right to keep.

Ariana Remington was asleep. In my bed. In our bed, technically, if you went by the marriage certificate I was keeping in my other hotel room.

I lay flat on my back, hands crossed over my chest like a man in a coffin, trying not to move. Trying not to *feel.*

And failing.

Because she was *there.*

Inches away, her back to me, the edge of the sheet sliding low over her bare shoulder blades. She'd changed into some silky black tank top and sleep shorts situation that had no business looking that good on someone.

She shifted slightly, and the sheet pulled tighter.

I looked away.

I had made a promise.

No touching. No flirting. No bullshit.

But lying next to her now—close enough to reach, close enough to remember every late-night whisper, every morning kiss, every brush of skin against skin—I felt like I was back in time.

Except now I knew how it ended.

I closed my eyes and counted backward from one hundred. It didn't work.

Instead, I remembered the first time we ever slept in the same bed. Her bedroom. Prom night. I'd snuck in the window at two a.m. I didn't sleep at all that night. Neither of us did.

God, we were so young. Nervous and stupidly in love. Both of us still virgins, both of us pretending we weren't terrified. But it hadn't been awkward. Not even a little. It had been…perfect. Slow and breathless and clumsy in all the right ways. She'd looked at me like I was her whole damn world, and I remember thinking, *This is it*. This is the girl. The only one who'll ever matter. I was right. Even back then, I was right. And somehow, I still managed to lose her.

The memory hollowed me out. Left me raw. Because lying here now, inches from her, I still felt like that same dumb kid—heart wide open, hoping like hell she'd look at me like that again. Like I was hers. Like we weren't buried under years of hurt and silence. I'd give anything to go back to that night, to that moment, before I screwed it all up. But time only runs one way. And right now, all I had was this: a sliver of closeness. A breath. A maybe.

I turned my head toward her. "You awake?" I whispered.

Silence. A long pause.

Then, soft as a secret: "Barely."

I smiled into the dark. "Can't sleep either."

"Shocking," she muttered.

"I keep thinking I should say something."

"Silence is golden."

Pause.

More silence.

And then, softer still, she asked, "What would you say if you did say something?"

I swallowed hard.

"That I never forgot what this feels like," I whispered.

She didn't respond.

"And I missed it," I added.

Still no answer.

"I missed *you.*"

Finally, her voice again—dry and razor-edged, but quieter than before. "Words don't fix what you broke, Christopher."

My phone buzzed on the nightstand. I glanced over.

Liam:

> Where the hell are you?

I texted back without thinking:

> With Ari.

A second later, three fire emojis popped up.

I rolled my eyes and flipped the phone over, screen down. Not now.

"I know." I shifted onto my side to face her back. "But I wanted you to know I *know.*"

She was still for so long I thought maybe she'd fallen asleep again.

Then—

"You left," she said, her voice like glass. "And I waited. I waited to hear from you. A call. A message. Something to tell me you made a terrible mistake. But it never came."

I sat up slightly, guilt crashing over me like a wave. "I thought staying away was the one thing I could do right."

"It wasn't," she said.

We were quiet again. And it killed me.

"Why now?" she asked after a long beat. "Why try now?"

I took a breath.

Because I don't dream about anyone else. Because the moment I've had one too many, your name is the only one I say. Because I still write songs about you and lie to the press when they ask who they're about.

But all I said was, "Because I finally realized I was wrong. About everything."

Her voice was barely audible. "That doesn't make it okay."

"I know," I said. "But I'm not asking for okay."

I reached out—*almost*—but stopped an inch short.

My hand hovered above the space between us. Warm air. Unspoken words.

"I just want you to know that if there's any part of you that still wonders if we could ever make it work again…I'm still here."

She didn't answer.

But she didn't move away either.

And for tonight, that was enough.

CHAPTER 25

Saturday just before sunrise — Ariana

I woke up warm.

Wrapped in heat and heartbeat and the faint scent of something I hadn't let myself breathe in for a decade.

Christopher.

His arm was around my waist. My back was against his chest.

And I was…relaxed. Which should've terrified me. It *did* terrify me. Because my first instinct wasn't to pull away. It was to stay.

My eyes opened slowly, the suite still shrouded in pre-dawn hush. The Strip was a blur of lights outside the window, but in here? Quiet. Steady. Safe.

I didn't remember how it happened—how we ended up tangled like this. I'd fallen asleep on the left side, facing away. We hadn't touched. I'd made sure of it.

But now?

His breathing was even. Asleep, maybe. Or pretending.

104

His hand rested low on my stomach, fingers splayed like muscle memory, like he *used to* hold me. Like he still knew how.

And worse?

So did I.

The worst part wasn't the feel of him, or the way my body hummed at the contact.

The worst part was that it felt *right.*

Like something I'd missed. Like something I hadn't let myself admit was missing.

I should have moved. Shoved him away. Made a dramatic exit with blanket tossing and a scathing one-liner.

But I didn't. I stayed. For just one minute. For just a few more breaths.

I stared out the window, into the blur of a city that never slept, and let my body remember the way it used to feel to be loved.

Because for all the damage… There had been love too. Epic, fierce, one-of-a-kind love.

He hadn't just been my boyfriend. He'd been my *home.*

And now he was a mistake with a marriage certificate and a dangerously good memory for where I used to like to be kissed. I could feel it.

His arm tightened slightly. Muscles flexing. Just enough to make me inhale. Just enough to make me want to lean back.

I closed my eyes again. Just for a second. Just to see if it felt the same.

It did.

And that scared me more than anything.

Because maybe I wasn't as immune as I thought.

Maybe, just maybe…

I didn't *want* to let go.

Saturday — Christopher

When I woke up, she was already gone.

Not gone gone. Just...standing by the window, fully dressed in black leggings and a T-shirt, arms crossed, hair pulled back like she was preparing to prosecute the entire hotel for emotional crimes.

But I saw it.

The way she was staring out at the skyline like it owed her something. Like she was furious she'd ever let herself sleep next to me again.

But she *had.*

And more than that—she hadn't run the second she woke up.

She'd stayed. Even if just for a moment. Even if she hated herself for it now.

I pushed myself up in bed, rubbing a hand over my face. "You know you snore, right?"

She didn't turn. "Nope. You were dreaming."

"Was I?"

"You said my name."

I paused.

"And then you wrapped your arm around me," she added, still not looking at me. "Which is clearly a violation of the no touching clause in our very legally binding forty-eight-hour contract."

I let the smile tug at my mouth. "Sue me."

She finally turned.

And yeah—her walls were back up. But there was something *underneath* them this morning. Something that hadn't been there yesterday.

She looked…shaken. Not broken. Not weak. Just slightly less bulletproof than usual.

"I should be mad," she said, folding her arms tighter. "I should be livid."

"You still can be," I said, climbing out of bed and grabbing a T-shirt. "I've got time."

She ignored the joke.

"I woke up," she said, "and for a second, I forgot how mad I was."

I didn't say anything.

"I forgot everything. College. The breakup. The years in between. For three whole seconds, I thought we were just… us." Her voice was brittle. "And then I remembered," she added quietly.

I crossed the room slowly, not touching her. Just close enough for her to feel me.

"I'm not trying to erase the past, Ari."

"Good," she snapped, voice sharpening. "Because you *can't*."

"I know." I nodded. "I don't want to go back."

Her brow lifted. "No?"

"I want to start over."

She laughed, short and joyless. "Start over? We're *married.* There's no over to start from."

"Then maybe we don't start over," I said. "Maybe we keep going. From right here. Right now."

She stared at me.

I met her gaze and didn't blink. "You can pretend last night didn't mean anything," I said, voice low. "You can file your papers tomorrow and tell yourself it was just a glitch in your otherwise perfect judgment..." I paused. "But we both know it wasn't."

Her eyes flicked away. She didn't deny it. It was another crack. A small one. But it was there. And I wasn't going to waste it.

"We've got twenty-four hours left," I said. "Let's see what happens."

She didn't answer. Didn't smile. Didn't melt. But she didn't leave either.

She stood there by the window, silent. Thinking. And I knew I'd made another dent in that wall.

One more push. One more day. And I might just break it open.

CHAPTER 27

Saturday — Ariana

The thing about emotional boundaries is that when one gets breached, the others start to look suspiciously flimsy.

I needed new rules. Stronger ones.

The kind written in stone, notarized, laminated, and possibly tattooed across Christopher's abs just to make sure he didn't forget.

Because waking up wrapped in him had felt good. Too good. Dangerously good.

The suite had been a mistake. A reckless, emotional landmine I'd stepped on with both feet. I told myself it was about boundaries. About proving I could coexist with him, stay detached, be *professional.* But the second the door had shut behind us, I'd known better. Sharing a bed with Christopher wasn't harmless proximity—it was suffocating. His breathing in the dark, the familiar smell of his skin, the way his body heat seeped across the mattress like it remembered mine... It was devastating. Every second chipped away at the walls I'd spent years fortifying. And the worst part? I'd put myself here. Voluntarily. Like an idiot who thought playing with matches wouldn't burn.

I needed to course-correct *immediately.*

"New terms," I said flatly, pouring myself hotel coffee like it wasn't a direct insult to caffeine.

Christopher looked up from the couch, still barefoot, hair sleep-ruffled, wearing a T-shirt that should be illegal on someone with biceps and that much nerve.

"Terms?" he repeated.

"Of our agreement," I clarified, sitting at the table with my laptop open but untouched. "Clause 1: No sleeping in the same bed."

He raised an eyebrow. "Little late for that, don't you think?"

"That was a breach. You're on thin ice."

He smirked. "Is that official legal language?"

"Clause 2: No confessions, real or implied."

His brows shot up. "You want me to lie to you?"

"I want you to stop trying to be the Christopher you were before you left me. That version of you died in a dorm room hallway eleven years ago."

That shut him up.

Good.

I wasn't trying to be cruel. I was trying to survive.

"Clause 3," I continued, steadying my voice, "No touching. We didn't touch last night."

"You sure about that?"

My eyes snapped to his.

Smug. Infuriating. Smirking like the memory of me pressed against him was his new favorite hobby.

I glared. "Accidental contact does not constitute touching."

He held up his hands. "Hey. You're the expert."

"And finally—Clause 4: No more almost kisses. No more tension. No more wandering gazes or shirtless proximity or soft-voiced declarations that make me question everything I've built since you left."

His expression softened. And that pissed me off even more. Because he looked like he understood. Because he *always* looked like he understood.

"Got it," he said quietly. "All clauses acknowledged. Terms accepted."

I narrowed my eyes. "You're agreeing too easily."

"I'm playing the long game."

There it was again—that confidence. That certainty. That *Christopher-ness* that made me want to throttle him and kiss him in the same breath.

"I'm serious," I said.

"So am I." He stood, walked to the fridge, grabbed a bottle of water, and looked at me over his shoulder. "But just so I'm clear…no touching, no kissing, no flirting, and definitely no telling you I still love you?"

I sucked in my breath, then I froze.

He turned to me and smiled. But there was no smugness in it this time. Just something patient. And quietly devastating.

"Noted," he said. "Clause 5: don't say the thing I've wanted to say since the moment I saw you again."

He disappeared into the giant bathroom, and I stared down at my coffee. The warmth was long gone, but I drank it anyway.

Some habits were hard to break.

Just like him.

Because the worst part wasn't hearing he still loved me.

It was realizing I wanted to believe it.

CHAPTER 28

"Okay, Team Bachelor/Bachelorette," Meg said, clapping her hands as we all milled around in the lobby of the Neon Museum. "Time for the ultimate test of who-knows-who-best."

The museum staff was clearly flustered, trying not to gawk at the actual celebrities in their midst. One teen in a neon windbreaker whispered, "That's Christopher Wentworth," like it was a sacred revelation.

"Should've just called it *The Newlywed Game*," Liam muttered, stretching his arms behind his head.

"We did!" Meg grinned. "But certain people got weird about it."

Certain people meaning *me*. Not that she'd said my name. She didn't have to.

Jeremy slung an arm around her shoulders. "We tweaked it. Now it's Team Bride versus Team Groom. Bragging rights and free drinks for the winners."

To make it fair, Meg had sent around a get-to-know-you

112

quiz the week before, one of those ridiculous group bonding things with questions like "What was your childhood nickname?" and "What's your favorite hangover food?" Everyone had filled it out—some more seriously than others—and now the answers were being used as part of the game. Which meant even the people who barely knew each other could play like they did. Instant intimacy, Vegas-style.

"Oh good," I said, dry as desert sand. "Nothing like high stakes to bring out our best behavior."

The staff ushered us into another VIP section—because apparently even museums had those. Hanging out with rock stars meant discovering new luxuries daily.

They'd gone all out: two long tables, buzzers, prizes—the full game show treatment.

It was supposed to be harmless. Fun. A group trivia game where we'd all answer questions about each other. Except, of course, Meg had insisted on randomized pairings.

Guess who I got paired with.

Courtney, the human spray tan, squealed, practically bouncing in her wedge sandals. "I got paired with Nick! This is going to be *so* fun."

And then—because the universe hates me—she turned to Christopher. "But I *wouldn't* have minded being paired with you. I have a feeling you're full of...surprises."

Her hand *lingered* on his arm.

I felt an unholy urge to stab her with a curly straw. One of those obnoxious ones shaped like a butterfly. Right through her perfectly contoured cheek.

I wasn't supposed to care. I wasn't supposed to feel this... *territorial.* But watching her paw at him, all glitter and giggles, made something sharp twist in my gut.

Christopher's gaze flicked to me. Just once. His mouth didn't smile, but his eyes did.

Smug bastard.

Haley sidled up to me. "So…what's it like waking up as Mrs. Wentworth? *TMZ* says it was super romantic."

I gave her a look that could freeze fire. "*TMZ* also once claimed Bigfoot was dating a Real Housewife. So."

She turned away and Christopher was right behind her. "Guess we're stuck together, Remington." He said it like an inside joke.

I adjusted my sunglasses atop my head. "Try to contain your disappointment."

"Never," he murmured.

Before I could come up with a scathing retort, Meg called us into place. The museum had set up a cute little quiz area, complete with clipboards and markers, beneath a towering vintage *Stardust* sign.

"First question!" Meg announced, grinning. "What's your partner's most irrational fear?"

I didn't even have to think.

"Easy," Christopher said. "She's convinced cheese curds are secretly alive."

"They *squeak*," I said flatly. "That's not irrational. That's suspicious."

Laughter rippled through the group, but when our answers matched perfectly, Christopher's grin turned softer. Almost…proud.

We kept going. Favorite movie? *The Princess Bride*. Worst high school job? *Hot dog vendor at Miller Park*. Secret talent? Mostly *fluent in Spanish, thanks to a summer internship in Panama.*

The answers came easy. Too easy. Eleven years apart hadn't erased a thing.

We weren't supposed to be good at this.

But we were.

When Meg tallied up the points at the end, she whooped.

"And the winners—by a landslide—Team Bride's very own Ariana and Christopher!"

Everyone clapped. Jeremy whistled. Courtney pouted.

I wanted to throw up.

The trophy was a ridiculous sash that said "Vegas Royalty." Jeremy shoved it into my hands with a grin. "You earned it, Ari."

But all I could feel was the weight of Christopher's gaze.

I needed out.

"Okay, I'm done. Time to head back to the hotel," I said, handing the sash to Ellie like it was radioactive.

Meg frowned. "But we were going to—"

"Have fun. Really. I'm just...dehydrated. Probably. Definitely. See you later."

No one argued.

I turned to leave, heart hammering.

And then Christopher's voice—low, unreadable—followed me like a hook catching on the hem of my dress.

"You still know me, Ari. Whether you want to or not."

I didn't look back.

Because I didn't trust myself not to turn around.

CHAPTER 29

Saturday night — Christopher

I followed every rule today.

Didn't touch her. Didn't flirt. Didn't tell her I loved her—even though I thought it when she argued with a bartender over the appropriate gin-to-tonic ratio like she was cross-examining a hostile witness.

I kept my hands to myself this morning when we all walked through the Bellagio conservatory and she stopped to smell the orchids.

I didn't kiss her in the elevator when we both reached for the same button and her hand brushed mine and her breath caught like she *felt* it.

I followed every damn rule.

And it still wasn't enough.

Because she still pretended none of this meant anything. Like we were just riding out a stupid bet. Like she wasn't clenching her jaw every time I stood too close. Like she didn't notice the way her pulse jumped when I said her name low and quiet.

But I saw it.

I know her.

I've always known her. If that trivia game didn't prove it, I don't know what will.

It rattled her. I could see it. Which is why she bolted back to the hotel like something was chasing her.

But tonight we have our last dinner. With the group. She can't hide from me.

OUR TABLE AT SUPERFRICO—A restaurant so over-the-top it made the rest of Vegas look understated—was loud and chaotic. Neon everywhere. Velvet booths. Performers walking around in wigs and sequins, doing card tricks one minute, delivering pasta the next. It was pure Vegas weirdness.

Perfect for blending in.

Not so perfect when you're trying not to stare at the woman sitting across from you like she's your last goddamn meal.

Ariana was doing her best to ignore me. She was holding court with Meg and Ellie, laughing at something Liam said, twirling a ridiculously curly straw in her drink.

And then Courtney slid into the seat next to me.

Fantastic.

"You know," she said, leaning in like we were mid-seduction, "I think it's *so* cute that you're pretending to be married for a joke. I mean, commitment is sexy. Especially on you."

Ariana's head snapped up so fast it was a miracle she didn't get whiplash.

Courtney's hand landed on my arm. A little too familiar. A lot too much. I saw Ariana's eyes narrow. Just a fraction. But enough.

Showtime.

I leaned back, giving Courtney a polite smile. "It's not really pretending."

Courtney giggled. Actually giggled. "Sure, but it's Vegas! What happens here—"

"Doesn't stay here," Ariana cut in, sliding into the seat on my other side like she belonged there.

She shot Courtney a smile so sharp it should've come with a warning label. "Christopher's *very* committed. Aren't you, darling?"

The endearment was a shot across the bow. And I'd never heard anything sweeter.

"Completely," I said, matching her tone. "For better or worse."

"For richer or poorer," she added, crossing her legs. Her bare knee brushed mine. Not an accident.

Courtney's smile wobbled. "Well. Aren't you two just adorable?"

Ariana sipped her drink, eyes never leaving mine. "We try."

Meg called Courtney's name from the other end of the table, and bless her for it. Courtney flounced away, leaving a cloud of flowery body spray in her wake.

Ariana swirled the ice in her glass. "You didn't need rescuing, did you?"

"Not in the way you think." I let my gaze drop to where her dress—red tonight, because she was trying to kill me— cut across her thigh. "But I'm not complaining."

"That wasn't jealousy," she said breezily. "It was self-preservation. I can only take so much vapid in my personal space."

"Mmm." I leaned in closer. "So you weren't picturing stabbing her with that curly straw?"

Her lips twitched. "That would be undignified."

"I won't tell."

We were so close now. Her leg pressed against mine. Her shoulder brushing my arm. Casual. Coincidental. *No way.*

"Do you know what I was thinking though?" she asked, voice low.

"What?"

She tilted her head, feigning innocence. "That you looked…bored."

"Maybe I was just waiting for someone to make it interesting."

"Careful." Her smile was pure trouble. "You're flirting. Clause Two violation."

"Technically, you started it. And speaking of violations, you're touching me." I stared down at where our shoulders met.

She didn't deny it, just slowly pulled away an inch.

The conversation swirled around us—laughter, stories, toasts—but for those few minutes, it was like we were back in our own little orbit. The way we used to be. Trading jabs and daring each other closer.

"Tell me something," I said, dropping my voice so only she could hear. "Did it bother you? Seeing her hand on me?"

She sipped her drink slowly. "Why would it?"

"You tell me."

"I don't care what you do, Christopher."

I leaned in, close enough to feel her breath. Close enough to smell her perfume, which was driving me insane. "You're a terrible liar, Ari."

Her pupils dilated. Her lips parted. But before she could retort, the server arrived with a round of shots and the moment broke.

Ariana turned away, tossing back her drink like she needed the burn.

But she didn't move her leg. And I didn't stop smiling.

Because I'd seen it. Felt it.
She wasn't nearly as unaffected as she wanted to be.

CHAPTER 30

Same time — Ariana

It was the curly straw's fault.

That and Courtney's acrylic-tipped fingers draped across Christopher's arm like she'd personally reserved the right to touch him. She was purring at him. Actually *purring*. I half-expected her to start making biscuits on his bicep.

And Christopher—damn him—was just sitting there, all casual charm and effortless patience. Not encouraging. Not shutting it down either.

My drink was sweating in my hand. I might've been sweating too.

Not because of Courtney.

Because of *me*.

Because seeing her touching him, smiling at him, sliding into his space like she belonged there—did make me want to stab her with my curly straw.

That wasn't part of the plan.

I wasn't supposed to care. This whole Vegas mess was temporary. Legal housekeeping. A detour.

But my body hadn't gotten the memo.

So I moved.

Right into the seat next to him.

Right into the blast radius.

He smelled the same. Soap and cedar and the faint, impossible echo of summer nights. Like the Midwest in July. Like reckless youth.

His leg brushed mine, and it was an accident the first time.

Not the second.

This isn't jealousy, I told myself. Lied to myself. *It's pest control.*

But then he smiled. That slow, knowing, dangerous smile that had been the undoing of so many of my good intentions. The one that used to make me forget curfews and study plans and every sane thought in my head.

And suddenly, I wasn't thinking about Courtney anymore.

I was thinking about how easy it would be to lean in just a little closer.

I could smell him now. We were so close. Warm, clean, expensive. My fingers twitched, aching to slide under his sleeve, to relearn the map of his forearm. To see if it still felt the same.

But maybe it wasn't. Maybe it was different now.

After all, my memories were from a girl. And now I was a woman.

Maybe it wouldn't be as good as I remembered. Maybe it would be disappointing. A letdown. A fitting coda to this entire disastrous weekend.

Or maybe it would be better.

The thought was an electric jolt low in my belly.

His arm brushed mine. I didn't move away. Couldn't. He laughed at something Luke said, low and rough. The sound went straight to my bones.

"I'm not going to bed with you," I whispered quickly, because it needed to be said. Because if I didn't say it out loud, I might do something very, very stupid.

"I didn't ask you to."

Liar. He'd asked me with his eyes, and we both knew it.

But when his fingers brushed mine—innocent, casual, bullshit—I didn't pull away. Neither did he.

We were back in dangerous territory. Old patterns. Old electricity.

His thumb stroked a line along the inside of my wrist. Barely there. But my pulse betrayed me. Jumped under his touch like it remembered everything we were trying to forget.

God, I wanted him.

Maybe it was the drinking. Maybe it was nostalgia. Maybe it was just Vegas doing what Vegas does.

But I wanted to go to bed with him.

To *remember*. To *test*. To *see*.

The rational part of my brain screamed that this was a terrible idea. That touching him, being near him, breathing him in like this—was emotional arson.

But my body had always been less reasonable.

"I'm violating the touching clause," he said, his voice cocky as hell.

"You are." I took a slow sip of my drink.

"Tell me to stop," he murmured.

I couldn't.

I didn't.

Instead, I traced my fingers up his arm, feeling muscle beneath my palm.

"You still fit me," I said before I could stop myself. "That's the problem."

"Maybe that's the answer."

I laughed, soft and bitter. "You always were a good talker."

"I'm better with action."

That earned him a look. A glare that wasn't as sharp as it should've been.

But the thing was…he wasn't wrong.

When his fingers threaded with mine under the table, it was like the last decade evaporated. Like we'd been paused—not ended.

Old times.

Old feelings.

New danger.

We stayed like that. Tethered by a touch. The world noisy and neon around us. But in that moment, it was just us.

And for all my big talk, all my laminated rules, all my righteous fury—my heart was beating to a rhythm I recognized.

Him.

Me.

Us.

Still.

Damn it.

CHAPTER 31

Vegas was loud, flashy, and demanding.

But next to Ariana, it was background noise.

We left the restaurant together, our group trailing behind, their laughter bouncing off the brightly lit sidewalks. The security guards were behind us, but it felt like we were in our own orbit. Every step, every glance was dialed in. Focused.

On her.

She walked fast, like speed would save her. Heels clicking, chin high, all sharp edges and stubborn pride. But her fingers twitched at her sides like they missed holding mine.

"You know," I said casually, falling into step beside her, "you were dangerously close to enjoying yourself tonight."

"That's debatable."

"You laughed, Remington."

"A reflex." She kept her eyes forward, but the corner of her mouth betrayed her.

"I'm very funny."

"Hmm. Questionable."

"Objectively funny, actually. Award-winningly charming. You should really check the stats."

"I don't need to. I've seen your fan girls." She gestured back vaguely toward Courtney. "Some of them are very... hands-on with their support."

I grinned. Couldn't help it. "Jealous?"

Her scoff was textbook denial. "Please."

"Your straw wanted blood."

"That was situational. Also, justified."

We crossed the Strip toward the hotel, weaving through tourists and street performers, the pulse of music vibrating up from the pavement. The lights reflected in her eyes, but she wasn't looking at Vegas.

She was looking at me.

"You were playing with fire back there," she said.

"I'm good with heat."

"Be careful, Wentworth. You'll get burned."

"Worth it."

She stopped then, one foot on the curb, one on the street, turning to face me with that look that always meant trouble.

"You think this is a game," she said quietly.

"No," I said, stepping in. Close, but not close enough to spook her. "I think this is a reckoning."

That got her.

For a second, her mask slipped. Her eyes flared.

But then she was moving again. "Thirteen hours left, Wentworth. Try to keep your existential crises contained."

"Not a crisis," I said, matching her stride. "More like clarity."

"Of course it is. Vegas is famous for it. People have epiphanies in strip clubs all the time."

I laughed, low and easy, because she was fighting and losing, and we both knew it.

The hotel loomed ahead, glass and steel and just a little too much symbolism. We reached the elevators, the group dispersing toward the casino and bars.

But not us.

Because we had unfinished business.

I nodded to the security guard who was following me. Telling him with no words that I wouldn't need him any longer tonight.

The elevator doors slid closed, and for the first time all night, it was quiet. Too quiet.

Ariana's reflection stared back at me from the gold-trimmed walls, all defiance and avoidance.

"I can feel you thinking," I said.

"Good. Maybe it'll rub off."

I didn't push. I didn't need to.

Because her pulse was thudding at her throat. Because her fingers flexed like she wanted to grab my shirt and shove me against the wall. Because the elevator was a pressure cooker, and we were both about to boil over.

Ding.

Our floor.

She stepped out first, head high, pace brisk.

But her shoulders were tight.

And when we got back into the suite, she slipped off her heels with a sigh. Her hair was a little windblown. Her mascara just starting to smudge. And she looked like everything I'd ever wanted.

"Twelve and a half hours left," she muttered again, heading to the bathroom.

"Still taking the money then?"

She paused. She didn't look at me, but her shoulders tensed. "That's the plan," she said finally.

I nodded. "Then I've got nothing to lose."

She turned. "What?"

I walked toward her slowly, deliberately. Not threatening. Just steady.

"Twelve and a half hours left," I repeated. "So here's what I want. One honest answer."

She crossed her arms. "To what?"

"To this." I stopped a foot away. "Do you still love me?"

She blinked. "No."

Too fast. Too practiced. Too false.

I stepped closer. "Say it like you mean it."

"I just did."

"You didn't hesitate."

"I didn't need to." But her voice was shaking now.

I took another step. "Say it again."

"Christopher—"

"Look me in the eye and tell me you don't still feel it. Tell me last night meant nothing. Tell me waking up in my arms didn't make you think, even for a second, about what it used to be like. About what it could still be."

Her throat worked. Her jaw tightened. She didn't say a word.

So I leaned in—slow, careful, a whisper from her lips—and said, "That's what I thought."

She didn't move. She didn't pull away. But her walls went up hard and fast.

"You don't get to do this," she said, backing up a step, her voice jagged. "You don't get to break me, then come back a decade later with sexy smiles and declarations and think I'll just forget."

"I don't want you to forget," I said. "I want you to remember. Because what we had? It was worth remembering."

"And it still hurts."

"I know," I said. "I live with that every day."

We stared at each other across a chasm that hadn't been

there twenty-four hours ago. Or maybe it had always been there. And we were finally facing it.

"I need a minute," she said.

I nodded. And for the first time since this all started, I walked away. Because the next move?

Was hers.

CHAPTER 32

One minute later — Ariana

I closed the bathroom door behind me like it could hold everything in.

It couldn't.

I stared at myself in the mirror. Red lipstick worn away. The faint shimmer of highlighter still clinging to my cheekbones. Hair barely hanging onto its bun like it, too, had had enough of this day.

I looked like a woman on the edge. Because I was.

Christopher's words were still ringing in my ears, low and sure and *true*. I hated that part the most. *Do you still love me?*

The answer in my mind hadn't been the one that had shot out of my mouth. Did I still love him? God help me, *yes*.

But that wasn't the question.

The real question—the one I'd been avoiding for eleven years—was: *Can I ever trust him again?*

Because loving him had never been the problem.

I'd loved him since I was sixteen and rolling my eyes at his silly jokes.

I loved him when he serenaded me under my window and wrote songs with my name in them.

I loved him when we were broke and messy and dreaming too much.

I even loved him the day he left.

And I hated that.

Because when he left, he didn't just walk out of my life. He walked out of our *future.* Without a fight. Without a chance. Without even asking what I wanted.

He made a choice for both of us.

And now here we were again. Another choice. But this time…it was mine.

Twelve and a half hours. That's what I'd said. Like I could hold out. Like I could keep him at arm's length with sarcasm and clauses and righteous fury.

But the truth?

I'd let him back in the second I woke up in his arms and didn't run.

And now, the idea of letting him go again—

That *hurt.*

Because what if this was it?

What if this *was* our second chance? The one we actually deserved?

My hands were shaking as I turned off the bathroom light and stepped back into the suite.

He was standing by the window, shirtless again—why always shirtless?—watching the Strip glow like a slot machine about to eat someone's soul.

He turned when he heard me. He didn't speak. Just waited.

And for once, I didn't make a speech. I didn't argue. I

didn't deflect. I walked right up to him, heart pounding like a trial verdict was coming in.

And I kissed him.

Slow. Certain. Like I meant it. Because I did.

He didn't move at first. Then his hand cupped my jaw, his thumb brushing my cheek like I was something breakable. Like he remembered exactly how I used to fall apart in his arms.

When I finally pulled back, he whispered, "That wasn't part of the rules."

"I don't care." I looked up at him. "I'm still scared."

"I know," he replied. "Me too."

"But I don't want to let you go. Not tonight."

He exhaled, shaky and slow. "Then don't."

CHAPTER 33

One second later — Ariana

The space between us vanished in a breath.

He didn't say another word. Didn't ask. Just bent down, slid his arms beneath my thighs and back, and lifted me like I weighed nothing. Like I was his.

My breath caught. My hands found his shoulders, anchoring me to him as the world tilted.

His grip was steady, strong. His chest brushed mine with every step as he carried me toward the bed. Every nerve in my body screamed alive.

I knew this body. Knew the curve of his shoulder, the heat of his skin, the low burn in his gaze.

But it felt different tonight.

More solid. Sharper. Hungrier.

When my back hit the mattress, the gasp that left me had nothing to do with surprise. His mouth was on me before I could think. Before I could doubt.

Firm lips. Rough stubble. That perfect scrape along my jaw, down my throat, making me arch into him. His hands pushed the straps of my dress aside, baring me inch by inch. No rush, no fumbling. Just reverence wrapped in possession.

He kissed my collarbone, my shoulder, each kiss claiming ground he'd never really lost.

The dress slipped down, pooling at my waist.

"Off," I breathed.

He obliged. He peeled the fabric away, slow, like unwrapping something he wanted to savor. Next went my bra. When it was gone, his hands paused. His gaze roamed every inch of me, hot and worshipful, making me burn.

"You're killing me, Ari," he said, voice rough. "You always have."

And then he was on me again. His mouth found my breast, tongue flicking, teeth grazing until my fingers tangled in his hair, tugging him closer. My hips shifted, restless, needy, but he took his time. Drawing soft, maddening circles with his tongue. Leaving me trembling.

I was gasping by the time his mouth moved lower.

Lower.

He kissed down my stomach, each press of his lips stoking a deeper ache. When he reached the edge of my panties, he hooked his fingers into the lace and met my gaze.

He didn't ask.

He didn't have to.

I lifted my hips, and he slid them down my legs, slow and deliberate.

The air hit me first—cool, teasing. Then his mouth replaced it.

One slow stroke of his tongue and my breath left me in a ragged exhale. He licked me with a patience that felt like torture, his hands gripping my thighs, keeping me exactly where he wanted me. I wasn't in control anymore.

And I didn't want to be.

My fingers fisted the sheets, trying to find purchase as he licked, sucked, worshipped.

It had never been like this with anyone else. No one else had ever taken me apart so completely. No one else had made me feel this much.

Pleasure built, sharp and unstoppable. I was right there, teetering, desperate.

"Chris—" His name fractured on my tongue.

He hummed against me, and that was it. I shattered.

My body arched off the bed, pleasure ripping through me in waves. I gasped his name again, a broken, helpless sound.

He didn't stop. Not until my thighs were trembling and my breath was ragged.

Only then did he rise.

His mouth was glistening. His eyes—dark and feral.

He kissed me, slow and deliberate, letting me taste myself on his tongue.

"Still think it won't be the same?" he whispered against my lips.

I dragged his jeans off in response.

His body was unfair. Broad shoulders. Cut abs. Muscles that flexed beneath my palms as I explored him like it was the first time. Like I had all the time in the world.

But I didn't want slow anymore.

I wanted *him*.

Now.

"Briefs. Off," I ordered.

His grin was sin incarnate.

"Yes, ma'am."

He shucked them with zero finesse. And then he was there, above me, hard and ready. He stroked himself once, slow and shameless, and my breath caught.

He lined up at my entrance, his tip teasing me, and paused.

"Ariana."

The way he said my name—hoarse, reverent—made my heart twist.

I reached for him, wrapping my legs around his waist. "Don't make me beg."

That was all it took.

He thrust into me in one smooth, claiming stroke. Filling me completely. Stretching me until the breath left my lungs.

My fingers dug into his back as he set a rhythm, each thrust deeper, harder, relentless.

We didn't talk. We didn't need to.

Every movement was a conversation. Every grind of his hips was an apology. Every brush of his lips against my skin was a plea.

His pace quickened, our bodies slick with sweat, the sound of skin against skin filling the room. I clung to him, nails raking his shoulders, hips meeting his thrusts with equal urgency.

I couldn't get close enough.

He couldn't get deep enough.

He rolled, pulling me on top of him, his hands gripping my hips as I took over, riding him with a desperation I couldn't hide.

I watched his face as I moved. Watched the way his jaw clenched, the way his hands flexed, the way his gaze devoured me.

"You feel so fucking good," he ground out.

"So do you." The words were a breath, a confession, a surrender.

His thumb found my clit, circling just right, and I fell apart again.

This one was different.

Sharper.

Deeper.

It left me gasping, trembling, collapsing against his chest.

But he wasn't done.

He flipped us again, driving into me harder, his rhythm brutal, his control unraveling.

I wanted to crawl inside his skin.

To lose myself in him.

When he came, it was with a groan that sounded like my name was the only word he knew.

He buried himself to the hilt, holding me so tight I could barely breathe.

But I didn't want to breathe.

I wanted to feel.

We stayed tangled together, panting, hearts racing, bodies sated but minds spinning.

And that's when it hit me.

If I'd been hoping this would be a pale imitation of the past—if I'd wanted proof that it was just nostalgia, that I could survive him again—I'd been wrong.

It wasn't the same.

It was better.

Richer. Rougher. More.

Because I wasn't a girl anymore.

And he wasn't a boy.

We were adults with scars and regrets and unfinished stories.

And right now, in this bed, in this moment, we made something new.

The tears stung before I could stop them.

He noticed.

Of course he did.

His thumb brushed my cheek, catching the first tear as it fell. He didn't say a word. Just held me.

And for once, I didn't pull away.
Because if loving him had always been the problem…
Maybe loving him was also the answer.

138

CHAPTER 34

Sunday morning — Christopher

I didn't sleep. Not really. Not with her next to me. Not knowing what morning would bring.

Ariana sat on the edge of the bed now, wrapped in the sheet like armor, hair tangled, spine straight. She hadn't said a word in fifteen minutes. Just stared out at the skyline, blinking slow, like maybe it would rearrange itself into something that made sense.

I slid our marriage certificate across the bed to her. I'd slipped out after she fell asleep and brought it back with me.

She picked it up. But she didn't open it.

"You remember our wedding?" she asked finally, her voice low, a hint of a smile.

"Every second," I said.

She looked at me over her shoulder, jaw tight. "Tell me."

"I walked you into the chapel. You kicked off your last heel halfway up the aisle and told the officiant to 'make it quick before I lose my nerve.' You laughed through the whole thing. Said marrying me might be the worst decision you'd

139

ever make—and then you looked at me and said, 'But it also might be the best.'"

She blinked fast, once.

"And when it was over," I added, "you kissed me like you meant it. Like maybe—just maybe—you didn't want it to be a mistake."

Silence.

I let her sit with it.

"I hated seeing your name in those headlines," I said. "Like it was a joke."

"I hated seeing it too. But what scared me more…was how much of me wanted to make it real." Then she whispered, "I want to believe it."

I moved toward her, slow. Careful. "But?"

She looked at me then—really looked. And I saw it all.

Fear. Longing. Rage. Regret.

"But I don't trust you," she said. "Not enough. Not yet."

The breath I took felt like shards of glass in my lungs.

"Then let me earn it."

She shook her head. "It doesn't work like that. Trust isn't a debit card. I can't just swipe it again and hope it goes through."

I was going to back off. Say something measured. Give her space.

But then she reached for me.

Fast. Desperate. Real.

And suddenly her mouth was on mine, her hands in my hair, her breath all over my skin like she was drowning and I was the only air left in the world.

I didn't ask questions.

I kissed her back.

Hard.

The sheet slipped from her body as she climbed into my lap, leaving nothing between us but history and heat. God, I was starved for her. Every inch of bare skin she pressed to mine set a fuse I had no hope of controlling.

"This doesn't fix anything," she said, her voice a low snarl against my lips.

"I know," I said, tasting the truth in her mouth. "But it's real."

Her fingers threaded into my hair, tugging just enough to make my pulse jackhammer. She kissed me like she hated me. Like she loved me. Like she didn't know where one feeling ended and the other began.

I couldn't get enough.

I rolled us over, bracing myself above her, just looking. Drinking her in. Her dark hair spilled across the white sheets like ink. Her chest rose and fell fast, matching my own ragged breath. The sheet had slipped to her waist, baring the smooth curve of her breasts. The way she looked up at me—defiant, vulnerable, furious—was a punch to the heart.

"You don't trust me," I said. "But your body does."

Her breath hitched. For a second, her eyes softened. "I hate you for knowing that," she whispered.

"Hate me later." I dipped my head, kissing the hollow of her throat, the swell of her breast. "Right now, just feel."

Her nails bit into my back as I took her nipple into my mouth, swirling my tongue until she arched beneath me. Her thighs shifted, parting, inviting, and it was instinct to slide my hand lower, mapping every familiar inch until my fingers found her slick and ready.

"Fuck, Ariana," I groaned. "You're killing me."

"Good." She bit my shoulder, her hips rising to meet my hand. "You deserve it."

Fair.

But even as she said it, her legs wrapped around my waist, holding me there. Wanting me there. The past didn't stand a chance.

I slid two fingers inside her, slow and deep, watching her come apart for me. Her head tipped back, lips parted, a soft whimper escaping as she rocked against my hand. I'd never forget that sound. I'd dreamed of it too many nights.

She was gasping now, close, so fucking close, but stubborn as hell.

"Let go," I murmured against her ear. "Don't fight me on this."

Her laugh was breathless, wrecked. "I fight you on everything."

"I know." I thrust my fingers deeper, curling them just right. "But not this. Not here."

Her back bowed, a cry catching in her throat as she shattered, clutching my wrist like she couldn't decide if she wanted to pull me away or keep me there forever. I kissed her through it, slow and reverent, tasting every broken piece of her.

When she finally stilled, her breath hitched again. But this time, it wasn't rage or pride holding her together.

It was fear.

I didn't give her a chance to retreat. I hooked her leg over my hip, sliding home in one long, slow thrust. We both stilled. Breathing. Feeling. Remembering.

No one else had ever fit me like this.

Her fingers curled against my chest, not pushing, not pulling. Just *holding*. Anchoring herself in a moment she didn't want to believe in.

"This doesn't mean anything," she said again, but her voice cracked.

"Then let me show you what it could mean."

And I moved.

Long, deep strokes, setting a rhythm that had nothing to do with revenge or closure and everything to do with need.

With home. Her legs locked around me, hips meeting mine in a tempo that was frantic and devastatingly familiar.

The sounds she made—those breathy little gasps, the soft curses, my name falling from her lips like a confession—hit me harder than any song lyric I'd ever written.

It was too much.

It wasn't enough.

I kissed her like I needed forgiveness. Like maybe, if I loved her right this time, it would erase every mistake. My hand tangled in her hair, tilting her head, deepening the kiss as I drove into her, her body arching to meet every thrust.

"Say it," I whispered against her lips. "Say you still feel this."

Her nails scored down my back, leaving welts I'd wear like a badge. "I hate you."

"You don't." I caught her bottom lip between my teeth, making her gasp. "Not here. Not now."

"Don't tell me what I feel," she bit out, but she was breaking. I felt it in the way her hips moved faster, in the way her breath hitched on a sob she tried to swallow.

I kissed the corner of her mouth. Her jaw. The hollow of her throat.

"I love you, Ariana." The words broke free before I could stop them. Raw. Unapologetic. "I never stopped."

Her answer wasn't words. It was a kiss—hard and bruising—as she flipped us, straddling me, taking control the way she always had. She sank down on me, slow and deliberate, her hands braced on my chest.

Her rhythm was punishing. Relentless. Each roll of her hips a demand.

"Is this what you want?" she asked, breathless.

"It's what I've always wanted," I gasped.

Her fingers slid up my torso, curling around my throat—

not tight, not threatening, just *claiming*. Her eyes burned into mine, daring me to lie.

"You hurt me," she said. "You broke me."

"I know." My hands slid to her hips, guiding her pace. "But look at you. You're still here."

She shuddered, her breath catching as I thrust up into her, meeting her every move. Her walls clenched around me, pulling me closer to the edge. I could feel her shaking, feel her fight warring with the truth of what we were.

She leaned in, her lips brushing mine. "This doesn't fix us."

"I'm not trying to fix us," I breathed. "I'm trying to find us."

And when she came, it was with a sound I'd never forget —half sob, half surrender—her body trembling as she collapsed against me. I rolled us again, kissing her like I could pour every unsaid thing into her skin.

I moved faster now, chasing my own release, each thrust driving the point home.

You're mine. You've always been mine.

I spilled into her with a groan, holding her tight, forehead pressed to hers, breathing her in like it was the first time. Or maybe the last.

We lay there, tangled and breathless, the silence thick with everything we couldn't say.

Her fingers traced lazy patterns over my chest, her breathing slowly evening out.

"This doesn't change everything," she said, but her voice was soft now. No bite. No venom. Just a girl as lost as I was.

"I know," I said, brushing her hair back. "But it changes *something*."

We stayed like that for a long time. Her body relaxed against mine. My hand tracing slow circles on her back. The world outside didn't exist.

But Ariana Remington was a flight risk. Always had been.

And when I finally drifted off, lulled by the impossible weight of hope, I should've known better.

Because when I woke up—

She was gone.

Just a note on the pillow.

I need time. - A.

My chest hollowed out as I sat up, the sheet still warm from where she'd been.

And somehow I knew. She hadn't gone back to her room. She'd gone back to Milwaukee.

CHAPTER 35

Sunday — Milwaukee — Ariana

The first thing I did when I got home was unpack my suitcase.

The second thing I did was pour a glass of wine and pretend I hadn't spent the last forty-eight hours married to Christopher Wentworth.

I couldn't fly back with the rest of the group on the private jet. I just couldn't. I needed time. Meg and Ellie both texted me all day, asking if I was okay. All I could manage was a lame thumbs-up emoji.

They left around noon. After Meg and Luke had a reportedly awkward breakfast with their estranged dad who lived in Vegas.

None of their texts mentioned Christopher. I couldn't decide if that was a good or a bad thing.

BY THE TIME I walked into my office Monday morning, my armor was back on. Pencil skirt. Black heels. Hair in a no-nonsense bun that said "Your Honor, I object" before I even opened my mouth.

No one could tell I was unraveling. Which was good.

Because I wasn't ready to explain how I went to Vegas for my brother's bachelor party and came back with an emotional hangover, a legal spouse, and zero idea why I hadn't filed for an annulment yet.

I had the paperwork. Of course I did. Drafted it on the plane on the way home. Downloaded it and reviewed it twice.

But it just…sat there. On my desk. Mocking me.

Unsigned.

Untouched.

Unfiled.

And I had no idea why.

Scott asked about it. I told him the truth—that I had no idea what I was doing. He was kind about it. Said I should look him up if I ever found myself single and a little less confused. But we both knew that call was never coming.

Scott deserved someone who didn't hesitate. Someone who chose him without question. First. Always.

Christopher had texted. He'd called. He'd even left a voicemail that I'd listened to but couldn't bring myself to delete.

"I meant every word, Ariana. And I'd say it again. Just give me the chance. Or tell me where to write the check."

I didn't reply.

I couldn't.

Because if I did…I didn't know what I'd say. But I couldn't bring myself to send him the address for the charity.

And I knew I'd have to see him again in four weeks. At Meg and Jeremy's wedding.

There was no avoiding it. No backing out. No skipping the ceremony and pretending to have COVID.

Which meant I had four weeks to figure out what the hell I was doing.

Four weeks to decide if I was running away again…

…or running out of excuses.

I buried myself in work.

Hearings. Depositions. Trials. Coffee.

I stayed late.

I said yes to every assignment.

I told myself it was just life going back to normal.

But every time I passed the stack of papers on my desk, every time his name popped up on my phone, every time I closed my eyes and remembered the way he looked at me when he was deep inside of me—

I felt anything but normal. I felt like a woman on a ledge. Like someone who'd walked away from something *almost* perfect…

Because she didn't know if she deserved to try again. And because the last time she said yes to love, it broke her.

But this time?

I wasn't sure it would break me.

I was afraid it might just *fix* me instead.

And that was somehow even scarier.

CHAPTER 36

Three weeks until the wedding — Nashville — Christopher

I hadn't heard from her in eight days. Not that I was counting.

Okay—I was absolutely counting.

I'd sent three texts and left one voicemail. No calls after that. I wasn't trying to chase her. I was trying to give her space. Trying to be the version of myself she could actually *trust* this time.

But silence has a way of getting personal. Every day that passed without a word felt like a new kind of rejection.

And the worst part? I couldn't blame her. I'd earned every second of her doubt. But knowing that didn't make it hurt less.

Luke, Nick, and Liam were pretending not to notice I'd gone full moody-bass-player mode. Rehearsals for the upcoming tour were going fine, technically. But I hadn't written a new riff in weeks. The notebook I usually filled with lyrics was still blank. My guitar sat untouched in the corner.

I wasn't making music. I was just…waiting.

And the wedding was getting closer.

Meg had texted a few times. Casual check-ins. Nothing heavy. But I knew Ariana was radio silent with her too. She was circling the wagons. Figuring out what to do with the fact that she'd let herself fall back into something real.

And maybe didn't want to admit she didn't hate it.

I pulled out my phone and opened the message app.

Typed:

I'm still here. That's all. –C.

Didn't send it.

Deleted it.

Instead, I grabbed my guitar and sat on the edge of my deck, looking out over the Nashville hills, and tried to remember the sound of her laugh.

The real one.

Not the one she faked to prove she didn't care.

The one I'd heard in college, when I made her pancakes at two a.m. The one she let slip poolside in Vegas, when she thought I wasn't keeping score. The one I hadn't heard since the night she left.

I missed her.

Not in the dramatic, tortured-artist way. In the practical, aching, ordinary way that made coffee taste worse and mornings feel wrong.

Three more weeks until I'd see her again. And maybe she'd look right through me.

Or maybe—

Just maybe—

She wouldn't.

CHAPTER 37

Two weeks until the wedding — Milwaukee — Ariana

I had Christopher's name saved in my phone as DO NOT TEXT THIS MAN.

Helpful, in theory. Less helpful when I kept staring at my phone like it might ring if I blinked hard enough.

I hadn't replied. Not to his messages. Not to his voicemail. Not to the look I imagined on his face when he woke up in that hotel suite in Vegas and saw my note.

I'd told myself I needed space. That I was doing the smart thing. The rational thing. The emotionally bulletproof thing.

And now?

Now I just felt numb.

So when my phone buzzed and Jeremy's name lit up with a FaceTime request, I debated ignoring it. Then I remembered I was still his bridesmaid and ghosting the groom probably was a bad look.

I accepted.

"Hey," I said, trying not to sound like I was halfway to a panic spiral.

He grinned. "Hey, Ari. You look…"

He trailed off.

"Like a woman who made a huge mistake in Vegas and hasn't slept properly since?" I offered dryly.

He winced. "Was gonna say tired, but yeah, that tracks."

I flopped onto my couch, blanket still wrapped around my shoulders, even though it wasn't cold. "Please tell me this is about table assignments and not a surprise therapy ambush."

Jeremy's face softened. "Just checking on my sister. Who's been avoiding everyone."

"I'm fine," I lied.

He didn't even blink. "You're not."

I sighed. "I don't know what I'm doing, J. I thought walking away would make it easier. Cleaner."

"Did it?"

"No," I said. "It made it worse."

He nodded slowly, like he'd expected that. "You know I remember what it was like after he left back then."

I swallowed hard.

"You were a zombie that summer," he said. "Ice cream, sweatpants, watching *Legally Blonde* on loop like it held the secret to surviving emotional trauma."

"That movie *does* hold the secret," I said, voice weak. "It's perseverance and good hair."

Jeremy didn't laugh.

"I didn't think you'd ever get over it, Ari," he said gently. "And if I'm honest? I don't think *you* thought you would either."

I stared at him, heart lodged somewhere in my throat.

"I've watched you over the years," he continued. "With other men. The occasional date. That guy from law school. That accountant you brought to Mom's Christmas party."

"Bill," I muttered. "He brought his own spreadsheet to Secret Santa."

"Exactly," Jeremy said. "And not one of them ever made your eyes light up."

I blinked. "You were…paying attention to that?"

"I'm your brother," he said simply. "I notice things. And I noticed that ever since Christopher left, your heart hasn't been in it. Not with anyone else."

I didn't know what to say. So I said the only thing that felt true. "I was too afraid."

"I know," he said. "It hurt to watch. You building walls so high no one even tried to scale them."

I stared down at the frayed corner of my throw blanket.

"But seeing you in Vegas?" Jeremy's voice dropped. "Ari…I saw your eyes again. I *recognized* them. They were full of life."

Tears threatened. I blinked fast.

"He made you come alive again," Jeremy said. "And I think you know it."

I exhaled. Shaky. Quiet. "So now what?"

"That's not for me to answer," he said. "But you've got two weeks to figure it out before you're in the same room again. And I think you should ask yourself one thing."

"What's that?"

"Is fear a good enough reason to walk away from the one person who makes you feel like *you* again?"

I didn't have a good answer. And before I could say anything else, Meg's face popped into the frame over Jeremy's shoulder, her eyes wide with purpose. "Sorry to hijack your moment, but don't forget—Mitchell's next Wednesday at four. Final fittings. If you bail, you're wearing a burlap sack down the aisle. Love you!"

She disappeared just as fast.

Jeremy looked amused. "She's terrifying."

"She is," I agreed faintly.

"Think about what I said," Jeremy finished.

I nodded and hung up. But I didn't need to think about it. Because deep down, I already knew it.

No. Fear *wasn't* a good enough reason to walk away from the one person who made me feel like *me* again.

CHAPTER 38

Wednesday at four — Ariana

Mitchell's Fabric & Fine Tailoring occupied a suite in a strip mall, but what it lacked in glamour on the outside, it more than made up for on the inside. And it had a door that jingled like you'd just walked into a Southern debutante's daydream.

It smelled like lavender starch and faintly of lemon. Rolls of silk and lace lined the walls like royalty. There were antique dress forms and floor-length mirrors angled to catch every inch of your ego—or insecurity—depending on the day.

"Ladies!" Mitchell practically sang as we stepped through the door, fanning himself with a white linen handkerchief. "My beautiful bride brigade has arrived. I could just faint. Somebody catch me!"

He was slight, in his early fifties, wearing skinny white jeans, a hot pink tunic top, and a belt that sparkled more than Courtney's lip gloss. Ms. Julia Sugarbaker, his tiny Maltese, trotted at his heels in a coordinating pink neck scarf, pausing to give each of us a sniff and a silent judgment.

"Ms. Julia is in one of her moods," Mitchell said gravely in his fake-southern accent that Meg had warned me about before we first met him. "She bit a UPS man this morning. Just the pant leg, mind you. He deserved it."

"Hi, Mitchell," Meg said, beaming. "We're ready for our final fittings!"

"Mmm, final fittings. The last step before a bride loses her mind entirely," he drawled, waving us toward the back. He pulled the bridesmaids dresses off a rack and handed them to each of us before turning to the bride. "Meg, darling, you first. Let's see if this gown still makes me weep openly."

Ellie caught my arm as we followed behind. "You good?"

"I'm fine," I said.

"She's lying," Meg whispered over her shoulder.

"You can stop treating me like an orchid," I groaned.

"No way," Meg replied.

I sighed and shook my head.

Mitchell's shop was part studio, part stage set—floor-length curtains, a pedestal, mirrors, and a discreet champagne cart. He pulled Meg behind one of the curtains, but not before blowing the rest of us a kiss.

I took my dress into a smaller fitting room. Courtney and Haley, already buzzing with energy, had already put on their gowns and were flitting around the mirrors like hummingbirds.

"These dresses are seriously amazing," Courtney gushed, running her hands down the satin of the emerald-green bridesmaids gown. "I feel like I should be starring in Bridgerton."

She wasn't wrong. Meg, the history professor, had chosen gown designs straight out of the English Regency. Empire waists, long skirts. Really pretty.

"I just want my boobs to look this good in real life," Haley said, adjusting her bodice in the mirror.

"Well, that's what tailoring is for, sugar," Mitchell called from behind the curtain. "We make miracles happen with darts and divine intervention."

Ten minutes later, Meg stepped out in her gown, and I swear all five of us made some kind of involuntary noise. Even Ms. Julia gave a tiny yip of approval.

"Holy crap," Ellie whispered.

"You look like a queen who eats diamonds for breakfast," I said, clasping my hands together.

Meg turned slowly on the pedestal, eyes misty. "Okay, now I'm crying. Dammit, Mitchell."

"I live to emotionally wreck brides," he said with a flourish.

Once Meg stepped down and wiped her eyes, Mitchell clapped his hands. "Next! Ellie, you're up. You too, Courtney. Haley, you're after that, and Ariana, darling, let's save the best for last. You know that green does scandalous things to your coloring."

EVENTUALLY, it was just me and Mitchell, who flounced dramatically into my dressing room as I zipped up the gown.

"Let's see you," he said, perching on a tufted stool and fanning himself like a southern widow in a Tennessee Williams play.

I stepped out.

"Oh, honey," he said, hand to chest. "You're going to cause a riot."

"It fits, right?"

"Fits? Child, it sings. It confesses secrets. I'm questioning my sexuality all over again."

I laughed in spite of myself.

He stood, adjusted a pleat at my waist, and then leaned in conspiratorially. "So...are you really married to Christopher Wentworth, or was that just a very convincing Instagram fever dream I had?"

My jaw almost dropped. I arched a brow. "Meg warned me you were a gossip," I said, smoothing the satin over my hip.

Mitchell sighed. "Meg is not wrong. But I only gossip about people I adore."

"Then consider me adored in silence," I said lightly.

He pouted. "I suppose that means no exclusive scoop? Not even a hint? A little morsel?"

"You can say you saw me looking flawless in emerald and leave it at that."

He studied me for a moment, head tilted. "Alright. Fine. But I must say… If I was married to that hunk, I would not let him out of my bed for a single minute, so I'm questioning the validity of the entire tale."

I looked away, heart thudding.

"Okay," Meg said, freshly changed back into her street clothes and sweeping in with her clipboard like a woman on a mission. "We've got notes for everyone. Haley, your hem. Courtney, straps. Ariana—"

"Perfection," Mitchell interrupted. "Absolute perfection."

"Noted," Meg said, before touching my arm. "You okay?"

"Yeah," I said. Then, softer, "I think so."

"Good. Because in two weeks, you're walking down that aisle, and I need my best girl shining."

I smiled, just barely. "I'll try not to trip."

Ms. Julia Sugarbaker yapped approvingly. Or condescendingly. It was hard to tell with her.

We left an hour later with garment bags, lipstick smudges, and a whole lot of feelings I couldn't quite name.

But as I climbed into the car, one thought stayed lodged in my mind.

If I was married to that hunk, I would not let him out of my bed for a single minute.

No matter how hard I tried to forget, part of me still wanted to pull him back in and never let him go again.

CHAPTER 39

Meg and Jeremy's wedding weekend — Milwaukee —
Christopher

I wasn't nervous.

That's what I told myself when the plane landed. That's what I told myself when I checked into the hotel, when I rehearsed what I might say to Ariana, when I tried on my suit and hated every goddamn tie I brought.

I wasn't nervous.

I was *wrecked.*

Because she'd been silent for weeks, and I was out of ideas.

Vegas was supposed to break her open. Show her what we still had. And it did—for a second. A flash. Long enough to feel like maybe, this time, I hadn't lost her for good.

But then she left. And she hadn't said a word since.

Still, I'd said yes to this wedding. Yes to flying into her city, her turf, her world—because *she'd* be there.

And I had to see her.

Even if it killed me.

The ceremony was in a historic church downtown—high ceilings, candles, strings playing some modern Taylor Swift orchestral version. I sat on the groom's side of the church, watching Jeremy and Luke standing up at the altar, hands clasped in my lap, pretending I wasn't feeling like I might puke.

And then—

She walked in.

Thank God I was sitting because if I'd been standing, my knees would have *actually* buckled.

But holy hell. Her dress was deep emerald satin, the color making her eyes light up, the bodice hugging every curve like it had been sewn onto her body by angels with a grudge against me. Hair swept up, eyes sharp, lips painted pink like a dare.

And all I could think was: *I married that woman.*

Even if she didn't want me now. Even if I'd already lost her again.

I felt Nick nudge me. "Easy, man. You're drooling."

I ignored him. Because she looked at me. Just for a second. And I swear—*swear*—the whole world went quiet as she walked down the aisle with a bouquet of wildflowers in her hands.

There was something in her eyes. Not softness. Not forgiveness.

But something *alive.*

She looked away too fast, turned to take her place beside the other bridesmaids. But that second? That glance?

It was oxygen. It was hope. It was all I had left.

I didn't have a speech. I didn't have a plan.

But I had that look.

And if there was still even a *fraction* of something left in her…

I was going to find a way to reach it.

Even if it was the last thing I ever did.

CHAPTER 40

Wedding day — Ariana

I told myself it would be fine. That I could handle it.

It was just a wedding. Just one weekend. Just one husband-shaped complication in a church full of flowers and a white aisle runner.

But the second I stepped out from the vestibule, I knew I was in trouble.

He was sitting up front in a black suit, tailored within an inch of its life, platinum gray tie slightly askew, like he hadn't been able to concentrate long enough to fix it. Hair just a little messy, like he'd run his hands through it five too many times.

And when he saw me—*really* saw me—he flinched.

Not dramatically. Just the sharp inhale, the subtle shift like his body didn't know whether to rise or collapse.

I watched him grip the edge of the pew. Anchor himself. Pretend he hadn't just come undone for a second.

But I saw it. Worse?

I *felt* it.

Like a gut punch wrapped in velvet. Like the ache of something I hadn't let myself name in weeks.

And then our eyes met. For a heartbeat. Maybe less.

But everything stopped.

The strings. The whispers. The weight of the air.

It all went quiet.

Because that look—*his* look—wasn't just *you're beautiful* or *I miss you.*

It was *I remember everything.*

I tore my eyes away and took my place at the altar beside Ellie and Haley, smiling like my insides weren't actively trying to reorganize themselves.

As the wedding proceeded, I tried to focus on Meg, on Jeremy—on the vows, the flowers, the moment.

But I could feel Christopher behind me. I knew he was there. *Watching.*

And it unraveled me.

Because I hadn't wanted to believe that what happened in Vegas was real. I'd told myself it was heat and history and tequila and nothing else.

But the way he looked at me just now? That was not nothing. That was *everything.*

And it left me wondering—

What if I'd been wrong? What if walking away had been the mistake this time? What if love—the real kind, the big kind—wasn't supposed to make sense?

And what if I was finally ready to stop running from it?

CHAPTER 41

Meg and Jeremy's wedding reception — Christopher

The second the music shifted to something slow, I found her.

I'd waited all through the ceremony, all through photos, all through the cocktail hour filled with tiny appetizers and overly polite conversation. I'd held back.

Not anymore.

She was standing near the bar, talking to Ellie and laughing—God, that *laugh*—head tilted, wine glass in hand, looking like she belonged to another life. One I still wanted.

I walked straight toward her.

She saw me coming. Straightened slightly. Braced.

I didn't stop. I didn't ask. I just offered my hand and said, "Dance with me."

Her lips parted like she might say no. But she didn't.

She set down her glass, slipped her hand into mine, and let me lead her to the dance floor like it didn't cost her everything.

And then—

We were moving.

Slow. Quiet.

Her hand on my shoulder. Mine on her waist. The kind of closeness that wasn't about sex or history or tension—it was about gravity.

We didn't say anything at first. We didn't need to. Her eyes met mine, just for a second, then dropped. She looked tired—shadowed under the eyes, like sleep had been avoiding her too. When I pulled her closer, her breath hitched. I felt it in my chest like a ripple.

I could tell… That she wasn't okay. That *I* wasn't okay. That maybe this dance was the only place where either of us had made sense in a long time.

"You look beautiful," I said softly.

She didn't answer.

"I almost didn't recognize you," I added. "It's been weeks."

Her voice was tight. "You could've called."

My brows shot up. "I did."

"I meant *again.*"

I looked at her. "I didn't want to push you."

"You pushed me just by showing up."

"I had to."

Her eyes finally met mine. And something cracked.

"I'm tired, Christopher," she whispered.

"I know."

"Tired of being angry. Tired of holding on to hurt. Tired of pretending none of this matters."

"Then stop pretending," I said, voice low. "This is real, Ari. It always has been."

She didn't speak. But her grip on my shoulder tightened. Her body softened. And for a few perfect seconds, we weren't in a reception hall. We were in our own world.

"I never stopped loving you," I said.

"I know," she whispered.

"And I'll wait. As long as it takes."

She blinked. Swallowed. Then leaned her forehead against my chest.

And we just…danced.

No tension. No pretending. Just her. Just me.

And one dance that said everything we couldn't.

CHAPTER 42

That night — Ariana

The zipper on my bridesmaid dress stuck halfway down.

Of course it did.

I stood in my hotel room bathroom in my slip, wrestling with satin and shame and the echo of his voice in my head. *"This is real, Ari. It always has been."*

The irony wasn't lost on me. The wedding was in Milwaukee—my own backyard—but we'd all booked rooms at the fancy venue hotel. Safer than driving home after the reception, we'd said. Really, it was an excuse not to go back to real life just yet.

Now I was regretting it. Because it meant Christopher was here in this hotel tonight too.

In this building. In some room. Maybe still awake like I was. Maybe not. Maybe fast asleep without a care in the world.

God, I hated that I cared.

It wasn't fair. It wasn't *supposed* to still feel like this. I was supposed to be past him.

Above him. Beyond him.

I was supposed to dance, smile politely, pretend I wasn't unraveled by the way his hand rested at my waist like he still had every right.

But I *had* unraveled. On the dance floor. In his arms.

With every word, every look, every breath that felt too easy for two people who were supposedly broken beyond repair.

I sat on the edge of the bed, toes still aching from the heels I'd kicked off hours ago, hair loose now, makeup smudged. I looked like the girl who'd once slept beside him for years—and felt like the woman who still wanted to.

Don't make me want this.

That's what I kept thinking.

Because if I let myself want it again, I'd start to need it. And needing him? That had once destroyed me.

I reached for my phone. Opened my texts. His name sat there, unread.

I tapped it open.

> You didn't have to say anything tonight. That dance was enough. For me. Always has been.

I stared at it.

Closed it.

Then opened it again.

And typed: *I think it was enough for me too.*

I hovered over send.

Deleted it.

Then I tried again. *What happens if I stop pretending?*

Still too much. Still too raw. I set the phone down and

laid back on the bed. I stared at the ceiling and hated the way my chest hurt more now than it did when I left him in Vegas.

Because back then, it was clean. Final. Now it was messy. Now it was real.

And now?

Now I was still carrying around his ring. I opened my little silk purse, the one that matched my bridesmaid gown. The cheap gold ring sat at the bottom of the silky lining, taunting me. Why I had I slipped this in my purse before I left my house earlier?

I was still legally his. And still—

Stupidly. Dangerously. Undeniably…

His.

I pulled the ring out of my purse…and slipped it on my finger.

CHAPTER 43

Wedding night — Christopher

I didn't mean to knock. I meant to walk away. Tell myself that her eyes meeting mine across that church were enough. That the dance was enough. That the feel of her body pressed to mine, her forehead against my chest—*enough.*

But I couldn't. So I knocked.

Three short taps. Quiet. Just in case she didn't answer.

But she did. A crack in the door. A flash of her face.

Then—surprise. Not anger. Not exhaustion. Not fear.

Just…Ariana.

Messy hair. Clean face. That green satin dress halfway unzipped and sliding off one shoulder. And something unguarded in her eyes that undid me completely.

She stepped aside. No words.

I walked in. Closed the door and turned.

And then I saw it.

The ring on her finger.

My ring. Vegas gold and rhinestone, cheap and stupid and perfect.

On her hand like it belonged there. I stared at it. Not subtle. Not hiding it.

Just—*staring.*

She followed my gaze. And her breath hitched.

"I don't know why I still have it," she said quickly. "It's not—it doesn't mean—"

"Ari."

She stopped. I stepped closer. Held out my hand. Not for her.

For the ring.

"Let me see it."

She hesitated.

Then slowly, she held her hand out palm down, like it was fragile. Like *she* was.

I took her fingers gently in mine and traced the band.

"It fits," I said quietly.

"So do old habits," she whispered.

I looked up at her. Close now. Closer than I'd been all night.

"Why *are* you wearing it?" I asked.

Her eyes flicked to mine. "I don't know."

"Because you want it to be real?" I pressed.

A pause. A breath. "Yes."

"But you're still scared?" I asked next.

She nodded.

So did I. "Me too," I said.

She didn't speak. Just stared at me with that impossible look I'd never quite learned how to survive.

"But I want to be scared *with* you," I said. "Not scared *of* you. Not of us. Not anymore."

Her voice broke when she said, "I don't know how to do this again."

"That's okay," I murmured. "We'll figure it out."
"What if I break again?"
"Then I'll help you put the pieces back."
Silence. Tension. Everything buzzing.
Then—she leaned in. And her mouth met mine.

CHAPTER 44

Two seconds later — Ariana

He reached for me, thumb grazing the ring I hadn't taken off. And I shattered.

This was it. This was the moment. The boundary. The line between *before* and *now*.

Before, I ran. Now? I wanted to be caught. I think I always had.

"Still married," I said, breath shaky.

"Still yours," he answered, stepping into me like gravity.

And then his mouth was on mine—hot, hungry, unapologetic.

I kissed him back like I needed to erase the space between us. Like I could climb inside him and finally feel whole again.

My hands slid under his shirt and T-shirt, feeling the hard planes of his stomach, the tense stretch of muscle across his ribs. I tugged upward, and he stripped both off like they were in the way—because they *were.*

He pushed the dress off my shoulders and then unclasped

my bra with reverence. Then he dropped to his knees in front of me. "Let me look at you."

I stood there, bare to him from the waist up, breathing hard, nipples tight from anticipation and the cool air.

His gaze scorched me.

"You're more beautiful now," he said, voice hoarse.

"So are you," I said with a laugh.

Before I could react, he pressed a kiss to the center of my sternum. Then lower. And lower.

His mouth found my breast, tongue flicking, teeth teasing. I gasped, hand flying into his hair, anchoring him to me as he lavished attention on me like I was something sacred.

"Christopher," I whispered.

"I remember everything about you," he said, kissing the curve of my waist. "How you arch. How you sound. What makes your legs shake."

Somehow he managed to unzip the gown and it whooshed down my legs, pooling on the floor at my feet. He lowered himself farther and kissed the inside of my thigh, then looked up. "Can I?"

"Yes," I said, already breathless. "God, yes."

He slid my panties down my legs and pressed his mouth to me like a man possessed.

His tongue traced every inch of me, slow at first, then firmer, deeper, relentless. He licked, sucked, teased until my thighs were shaking and my voice was raw from moaning his name.

I came once on his mouth, and he didn't stop. He kept going. Brought me to the edge again, and this time I pulled him up.

"I need you inside me," I whispered.

He didn't speak—just stripped off his pants and boxers, his eyes never leaving mine. His cock was hard, thick, flushed at the tip.

He grabbed my thighs and lifted me. I wrapped my legs around his waist as he carried me to the bed and laid me down.

The second he pushed into me, I broke.

He filled me in one long, deep stroke, and I arched into him, breath caught on a cry.

"Jesus, Ari," he groaned. "You feel so good."

He moved slowly at first, hips grinding into mine, keeping eye contact like he needed to see every reaction. But then my heels dug into his back, and the pace shifted.

Faster. Harder. Deeper.

We were a tangle of limbs and sweat and noise. His mouth on my throat, my nails down his back. I kissed his shoulder, bit his lip, begged for more. And he gave it to me.

Over and over.

His thrusts got rougher, his rhythm frantic. I reached between us and rubbed my clit—once, twice—and we came together with matching cries. He held me close, his voice low and reverent, every word a promise against my ear.

He collapsed on top of me, breathing hard, his weight grounding me in a way I hadn't known I missed.

I held him there.

Let him stay.

Because I didn't want this moment to end.

And when he finally rolled onto his side, pulling me with him, he kissed my shoulder and whispered, "Still mine."

And I didn't deny it.

Because I was.

CHAPTER 45

The next morning — Ariana

Sunlight was creeping in.

Not in a dramatic, cinematic way. Just slow and steady—threading through the gaps in the blackout curtains like it had all the time in the world. The kind of morning light that didn't demand anything, just offered warmth and clarity.

I blinked against it and stretched, feeling the whisper of sheets against bare skin and the pull of muscles I hadn't used like that in longer than I wanted to admit.

And then I felt him.

His body, warm beside mine. The slow, even rhythm of his breathing. The weight of his presence in the bed—comforting, undeniable.

Christopher.

Still here.

I shifted slowly, trying not to wake him yet, and let my gaze drift over his face. The same one I used to watch in high school while he slept off late-night band rehearsals in my

177

twin-sized bed. Hair a mess. Lips parted slightly. His brow relaxed in sleep the way it never seemed to be when he was awake.

He looked…peaceful. Like maybe—just maybe—he wasn't waiting for the next fight or the next goodbye.

And the ring?

Still on my finger. Still warm from sleep and skin.

Not an accident. Not a leftover from some tequila-soaked joke. I'd had time to take it off. Time to change my mind.

But I hadn't.

I rolled onto my side and propped myself up on one elbow, watching him breathe. One of his hands lay relaxed on the sheet between us. The other curled beneath the pillow like a boy—not a man, not a rock star—but a boy I used to know. A boy who used to kiss me behind the bleachers and play songs he wrote just for me in the back of his dad's garage. A boy who used to fall asleep mid-sentence, my name still on his lips.

God, we'd been stupidly in love.

And now? I didn't know what this was. Not exactly. But it wasn't a mistake.

Not anymore.

Last night hadn't been about adrenaline or drama. Not about making a point or proving anything. After we made love—after I gave in to the pull I'd been resisting for weeks— we hadn't just passed out like a pair of teenagers.

We talked.

Laid there, tangled up in each other, the kind of close you don't fake.

He told me things I hadn't expected. About songs he wrote but never recorded. About the quiet panic of success— how you could stand in front of a stadium of screaming fans and still feel alone. He'd wondered, more than once, if I ever listened to his songs. If I ever thought about him. If I still had the bracelet he gave me after senior prom.

(For the record, I do. It's in a drawer. I haven't had the guts to throw it away.)

And I'd told him things too.

About court. About the pressure of trying to be someone who makes a difference. About how some nights, I stare at case files until the words stop making sense, and I wonder if I'm helping or just pretending. About how much I miss my dad. About how I'm up for Deputy District Attorney and not entirely sure I'm ready.

We didn't fix anything.

But we were real.

There were no stage lights. No wedding chapel. No vodka shots or Elvis impersonators. Just us. Raw. Unscripted.

This morning, I didn't wake up with regret clawing at my throat.

No shame. No panic. No scramble to run.

I felt…still. Present. Ready.

I reached for him.

Carefully, like I wasn't sure I had the right. My fingers brushed his, and for a second, nothing happened. But then his hand twitched. Turned. Closed around mine.

And his eyes opened.

A little bleary. A little tired. But warm. And clear.

"Still here," he said, voice low and rough with sleep.

I nodded. "Still married."

His mouth curved into a sleepy smile, slow and cautious, like he wasn't sure how much to hope.

"Still want to be?"

I let out a breath I hadn't realized I was holding.

Not shaky. Not scared. Just sure.

"I think I do," I said quietly. "I think…this time, I stay."

Something flickered across his face then—relief, maybe. Gratitude. Wonder.

He didn't speak right away. Just brought my hand to his mouth and pressed a kiss to the inside of my wrist. It wasn't a seduction. It wasn't a performance.

It was soft. Reverent. Real.

And I let him. Because this wasn't Vegas. This wasn't a joke, or a hangover, or a headline waiting to happen.

This was us. The real us.

Complicated. Broken in places. Still healing. But not finished.

He rolled onto his side to face me fully, our hands still clasped between us. "You don't have to promise anything yet," he said, his voice gentle. "You don't owe me that."

"I know." I traced the edge of his thumb with mine. "But I want to try."

A beat passed. Then another.

"I want the version of us that doesn't crash and burn," I added softly.

He exhaled. Closed his eyes like he was making a wish. "Then we try."

The light had shifted by now, casting golden streaks across the sheets and warming the air between us. He pulled me close, his arm wrapping around my waist like we'd never stopped being this—whatever this was.

I rested my head on his chest and let my eyes close again. Because for the first time in a long time, I didn't feel like I was bracing for impact.

I felt safe. Whole. Like maybe, just maybe, we'd finally figured out how to hold on without falling apart.

And maybe—maybe—we were only just getting started.

We were us again…finally.

EPILOGUE

One Year Later — Nashville & Milwaukee — Ariana

The thing about marrying your high school sweetheart in a haze of Vegas lights and tequila is that it *should* be the end of the story.

But with Christopher Wentworth?

It was just the beginning.

The tabloid headlines had faded. People moved on. Some still called it a publicity stunt. But when we filed for a real marriage license, no one could deny it anymore—we meant it.

We split our time now—Milwaukee for me, Nashville for him. I kept my job. He kept his band. We share a place in each city and a constantly updated shared calendar that includes things like *"virtual court date @ 2"* and *"album drop party."*

We're not perfect. But we show up. Every time.

Even when it's messy. Even when it's hard. Especially when it matters.

Like now.

Because right now, I'm sitting on the deck of Luke Knightley's giant house in Nashville, drinking lemonade and watching Meg cradle a tiny baby bump while Jeremy hovers nearby like she might sneeze and the baby will fall out.

"You're not fragile," I tell her.

"Tell him that," she mutters, shooting her husband a look.

"She walked into the kitchen barefoot yesterday," Jeremy says. "I almost called 911."

"You almost passed out," Meg corrects.

Christopher grins beside me. "Can't wait to see what you're like in the delivery room."

Jeremy blanches.

Meg smirks. "He'll faint. I've accepted it."

We're interrupted by the sound of a champagne cork popping and Ellie squealing as Luke lifts her hand in the air, flashing a *very* sparkly diamond to the table.

"We're engaged!" she announced, beaming.

There's clapping. There's shouting. Meg almost spills her ginger ale. Jeremy hugs Luke so hard it looks painful.

I just sit there and smile.

Because I already had my chaos. My elopement. My second chance.

And now, I have him.

Christopher pulls me closer, kissing my temple. "You okay?" he murmurs.

I nod. "Better than okay."

"Still married."

"Still want to be," I say.

He grins. "Good. Because I'm never letting you go again."

I smile back and my hand slides into his. I glance down to see the obnoxious ring he bought me after I decided to stay. It's nicer than the original, but I still keep that in my jewelry box too because I'm sentimental like that.

It's been a year since Vegas. A year since I stopped

running. And in that time, I've learned that home isn't a city. It's not a job. It's not a plan that works on paper.

It's a person. *My* person. Still mine. Finally mine.

Forever.

THANK YOU FOR READING. I hope you enjoyed Ariana and Christopher's story. It's the final book in the Austen Hunks trilogy. If you'd like to read more of my contemporary romance, CLICK HERE TO READ *The Honeycrisp Orchard Inn* now.

The Debutante Dilemma (Book 3)

The Wallflower Win (Book 4)

Lords in Disguise

The Footman is an Earl (Book 1)

Duke Looks Like a Groomsman (Book 2)

The Marquess Who Loved Me (Book 3)

Save a Horse, Ride a Viscount (Book 4)

Earl Lessons (Book 5)

The Duke is Back (Book 6)

Playful Brides

The Unexpected Duchess (Book 1)

The Accidental Countess (Book 2)

The Unlikely Lady (Book 3)

The Irresistible Rogue (Book 4)

The Unforgettable Hero (Book 4.5)

The Untamed Earl (Book 5)

The Legendary Lord (Book 6)

Never Trust a Pirate (Book 7)

The Right Kind of Rogue (Book 8)

A Duke Like No Other (Book 9)

Kiss Me At Christmas (Book 10)

Mr. Hunt, I Presume (Book 10.5)

No Other Duke But You (Book 11)

Secret Brides

Secrets of a Wedding Night (Book 1)

A Secret Proposal (Book 1.5)

Secrets of a Runaway Bride (Book 2)

A Secret Affair (Book 2.5)

Secrets of a Scandalous Marriage (Book 3)

It Happened Under the Mistletoe (Book 3.5)

I'd love to keep in touch.

- Visit my website for information about upcoming books, excerpts, and to sign up for my email newsletter: www.ValerieBowmanBooks.com or at www.ValerieBowmanBooks.com/subscribe.
- Join me on Facebook: http://Facebook.com/ValerieBowmanAuthor
- Join me on Instagram: http://www.instagram.com/valeriegbowman/
- Reviews help other readers find books. I appreciate all reviews. Thank you so much for considering it!

Want to read the other Austen Hunks books?

- Hiring Mr. Darcy
- Kissing Mr. Knightley
- Marrying Mr. Wentworth

ABOUT THE AUTHOR

Valerie Bowman grew up in Illinois with six sisters (she's number seven) and a huge supply of romance novels.

After a cold and snowy stint earning a degree in English with a minor in history at Smith College, she moved to Florida the first chance she got.

Valerie now lives in Jacksonville with her family including her two rascally dogs. When she's not writing, she keeps busy reading, traveling, or vacillating between watching crazy reality TV and PBS.

Valerie loves to hear from readers. Find her on the web at www.ValerieBowmanBooks.com.

facebook.com/ValerieBowmanAuthor

instagram.com/valeriegbowman

goodreads.com/Valerie_Bowman

bookbub.com/authors/valerie-bowman

amazon.com/author/valeriebowman